John Rushout Northwick

# Catalogue of the Late Lord Northwick's Extensive and Magnificent Collection of Ancient and Modern Pictures

Anatiposi

**John Rushout Northwick**

# Catalogue of the Late Lord Northwick's Extensive and Magnificent Collection of Ancient and Modern Pictures

Reprint of the original.

1st Edition 2023 | ISBN: 978-3-38230-577-2

Anatiposi Verlag is an imprint of Outlook Verlagsgesellschaft mbH.

Verlag (Publisher): Outlook Verlag GmbH, Zeilweg 44, 60439 Frankfurt, Deutschland
Vertretungsberechtigt (Authorized to represent): E. Roepke, Zeilweg 44, 60439 Frankfurt, Deutschland
Druck (Print): Books on Demand GmbH, In de Tarpen 42, 22848 Norderstedt, Deutschland

# CATALOGUE

OF THE LATE

# LORD NORTHWICK'S

Extensive and Magnificent Collection

OF

ANCIENT AND MODERN

# PICTURES,

CABINET OF MINIATURES AND ENAMELS,

And other Choice Works of Art,

AND THE

FURNITURE, PLATE, WINES, AND EFFECTS,

AT

# THIRLESTANE HOUSE,

CHELTENHAM.

Which will be Sold by Auction by

# MR. PHILLIPS

AT THE MANSION,

On TUESDAY, the 26th of JULY, 1859,

AND TWENTY-ONE SUBSEQUENT DAYS,

*Commencing at One o'Clock precisely each Day,*

BY DIRECTION OF THE ADMINISTRATOR.

May be Viewed on and after Friday, the 15th of July, by Catalogues only, at Five Shillings each, to admit Three Persons, to be obtained at the Lodge of the Mansion; of Messrs. AGNEW and SONS, Manchester; Mr. ISAACS, Liverpool; Mr. KERSLAKE, Bookseller, Bristol; Mr. HOLMES, Birmingham; Mr. BENTLEY, Worcester; Mr. DAVIES, Cheltenham; Mr. GREENWOOD, York; and at Mr. PHILLIPS' Auction Offices, 73, New Bond Street, London.

J. DAVY & SONS, Printers, 137, Long Acre, London.

## CONDITIONS OF SALE.

---

FIRST.—The highest bidder to be the purchaser, and if any dispute arise between two or more bidders the lot to be put up again and re-sold.

SECOND.—No person to advance less than 1s. at each bidding; above five pounds, 2s. 6d., and so advance in proportion.

THIRD.—The purchasers to give in their names and places of abode, and to pay down immediately a deposit of £20 per cent. in part payment of the purchase-money; and, if required, the whole of the purchase-money; or in default, the lot to be put up again and resold.

FOURTH.—The lots to be absolutely cleared away, with all faults and errors of description, at the purchaser's expense, within ONE DAY after each day's sale, without reference to the identity of either subject or master.

FIFTH.—*As this auction is made subject to the 4th condition, the remainder of the purchase-money must be paid on or before the delivery of the lots.*

SIXTH.—Upon failure of complying with the above conditions the money deposited in part payment will be forfeited, all the lots uncleared will be re-sold either by public or private sale, and the deficiency (if any), together with all charges for such re-sale, shall be made good by the defaulter at this sale.

LASTLY.—Should any purchaser obtain his lot or lots, and leave the same, or any part, uncleared, or by any neglect omit paying for the same, such purchaser shall pay interest after the rate of £5 per cent. per annum on the amount of the said purchase, from the day of sale until the amount shall be discharged, together with all charges attending such neglect.

# PREFACE.

In submitting Lord Northwick's very important Collection of Pictures to the competition of Purchasers, Mr. Phillips cannot omit the opportunity of respectfully calling the attention of Connoisseurs and Patrons of Art, to this, as one of the rarest occasions hitherto known in the annals of Auctions; combining, as it does, a Gallery exceeding Fifteen Hundred Pictures, enabling them from such a source to select works of the highest merit, both as regards the Ancient Masters, as well as those of the Modern English Painters. In the formation of the Catalogue, he has purposely avoided giving any lengthened or elaborate descriptions of the Pictures, although highly worthy of such encomium, believing as he does, that the beauty of each painting will be more satisfactorily appreciated by an inspection than from the recommendations of a *Catalogue Raisonné*, which he considers, at best, but a very inadequate medium, where works of such merit abound, as will be found in this Collection.

It may not be inopportune however to state, that in the formation of this Collection the late noble Owner's early and long cherished love of Art, aided by the most refined taste, which continued during a period of more than sixty years, enabled him to secure, from the numerous sources which have arisen in England and on the Continent, the present magnificent Collection now adorning the walls of THIRLESTANE HOUSE, and in quoting two paragraphs from a letter addressed by his Lordship, in reply to a testimonial which was presented to him by upwards of seven hundred Noblemen and Gentlemen of the Town and neighbourhood of Cheltenham, Mr. PHILLIPS feels that he may leave the interests of this important Sale in the hands of the Public—assured as he is that a visit to the galleries of THIRLESTANE HOUSE before they are dispersed, will afford ample satisfaction.

"I had myself the good fortune to commence my travels through foreign lands at an early period of my life, and it was in the year 1792 that I first saw Rome, where I sojourned during the greater part of eight successive years, and was impressed with a profound veneration—which, during the whole course of a long life, has never since been effaced from my memory—for the stupendous monuments of falling greatness with which it is on all sides surrounded—an unbounded admiration for the works of the most refined art in painting, sculpture, and architecture, with which it then abounded, and to which I had the advantage of a most free and unlimited access.

"These were the seductive amusements of my youth; they have clung to me through a long life, and they are now the solace of my old age. That they have not been a selfish and egotistic pursuit is abundantly testified by the kind feeling that has prompted so many of my highly respected friends and neighbours to present me with this invaluable testimonial of their approbation and regard."

# CATALOGUE

OF

# THE PICTURES AND WORKS OF ART

AT

## Thirlestane House, Cheltenham.

---

## FIRST DAY'S SALE.

On TUESDAY, the 26th day of JULY, 1859,

AT ONE O'CLOCK PRECISELY.

---

## DRAWING ROOM.

LOT

KIDD.

1 The Irish Wedding.

G. ROMANO.

2 Apollo and the Nine Muses.

A. CARACCI.

3 Portrait of Piovano Arlotto.

LIVERSEGE.

4 Don Quixote.

GAINSBOROUGH.

5 A Cottage Scene, with cattle and figure.

## CLAUDE.

6 An Italian Landscape, commanding a View of a Bay; on the right a Temple, near which an artist is seated sketching; a little to the left in the foreground a group of four figures.
*The effect of sunset is admirably rendered.*

## A. CARACCI.

7 A Portrait of a Man in a black dress.

## TIEPOLI.

8 Coriolanus receiving the Roman Matrons. *A powerful sketch.*

## R. WILSON.

9 A Landscape, sunset; in the foreground a peasant in a red dress, and in the distance a group of cattle.

## STOOP.

10 The Battle of the Bridge.
*Painted with great spirit and force of colouring.*

## JAN STEEN.

11 The Village School. *A humorous picture.*

## CARAVAGGIO.

12 A Student and his Pupil. *Painted with great force and expression.*

## SALVATOR ROSA.

13 A Rocky Landscape—A View near the Bay of Salerno; in the foreground are three figures standing out in fine relief.

## BOLOGNESE.

14 A Grand Landscape, in which is introduced the Story of the Rape of Proserpine.

## HOBBIMA (SCHOOL).

15 A Landscape with a mill pond, and a man shooting at some ducks; to the right a road with a peasant driving cattle.

## VENETIANO.

16 The Holy Family with Saints.

## RAFFAELLE (SCHOOL).

17 The Massacre of the Innocents.

## A. VANDER NEER.

18 A River Scene in Holland, by moonlight, with numerous figures, cattle, boats and buildings.

## J. DE HEEM.

19 A Group of Fruit, with lobster and silver vase. *Capitally painted.*

## ALBANO.

20 A Mythological Subject.

## DE KONINGH.

21 Cattle and figures on the banks of a river.

## CLAUDE.

22 A Landscape with a river running through the centre, traversed by a bridge; in the foreground is represented the Repose of the Holy Family.

## VAN SON.

23 A Group of Fruit and Still Life.
*Signed and dated* 1660. *Brilliantly painted.*

## J. AND A. BOTH.

24 A Mountainous Landscape, with peasants and cattle travelling along a road; in the foreground a group of figures reposing.

## PADUANINO.

25 The Virgin with the Infant Saviour seated in a landscape.

## A. CUYP.

26 A Landscape with a group of five cows, one of which is drinking at a stream.

## NICCOLO DEL ABBATI.

27 The Holy Family with the Virgin in Adoration.

## ALBANO.

28 A Landscape with Apollo in pursuit of Daphne.
*A charming composition.*

## PALMEZZANO.

29 The Virgin and Infant Saviour attended by St. Peter and St. Catherine, and an Angel presenting fruit; a rocky landscape is seen in the background.

*A fine composition—admirably coloured.*

## SALVATOR ROSA.

30 A Rocky Scene, with two figures in the foreground.

*Purchased by Lord Northwick from the Collection of Sir T. Lawrence, by whom this fine work was greatly prized.*

## ALBERT CUYP.

31 A Landscape with a group of three cavaliers halting at the door of an inn, near them a woman holds a jug; in the distance a river with a church and other buildings, and on the bank, suttler's booths, figures, horses, &c. *From the Boursault Collection.*

## M. HOBBIMA.

32 A richly Wooded Landscape, with a stream in the foreground, and two figures fishing.

*A pure and beautiful example of the master.*

## JAN BELLINI.

33 The Virgin with the Infant Saviour; a landscape with some buildings is seen in the background; *signed.*

*A beautiful example of the master.*

## JACOB RUYSDAEL.

34 A Forest Scene, with a rushing waterfall in the foreground, and two men angling.

*This picture possesses all the vigour and grandeur of effect for which its painter is so distinguished. It is engraved.*

## J. VAN HUYSUM.

35 A Landscape with Diana and her Nymphs.

*Very highly finished, and brilliant in colouring. On Copper.*

## NIEULANT.

36 A rocky Landscape, with the Flight into Egypt introduced.

## VANDER NEER.

37 View on a River in Holland, with numerous buildings, boats and figures; in the foreground a man fishing. Twilight scene.

## VANDER HEYDEN.

38 View of the Town of Nemiguen, with figures by A. V. Velde.
*From the collection of Van Lankers of Antwerp.*

## WYNANTS.

39 A View on the Rhine, representing wild and picturesque scenery, with a hilly country on the left; enriched with figures and cattle by Lingleback.

## G. POUSSIN.

40 An Italian Landscape, with two figures in the foreground.

## NICHOLAS BERGHEM.

41 A rich Mountainous Landscape, with a distant view of a city and the Lake of Peruggia; in the foreground a group of peasants are driving their flocks and herds from market; a threatening sky, denoting an approaching storm, gives grandeur and effect to the picture.
*An important and beautiful work of the master; signed and dated* 1653.

## J. RUYSDAEL.

42 A Wooded Landscape, with a cottage to the left, and a pool of water in the foreground; in the centre of the picture two peasants are standing in conversation.

## D. TENIERS.

43 A Landscape, with figures at a table drinking in front, while others are playing at skittles at a distance.
*From the Earl Spencer's collection at Althorp.*

## SASSO FERRATO.

44 The Virgin, with her hands clasped, looking attentively on the Infant Saviour asleep. *Charmingly coloured.*
*From the same collection as the preceding picture.*

## PLATZER.

45 The Battle of Amazons, a composition of numerous figures, finished in all its details with the greatest minuteness.

## VAN KESSELL.

46 A richly Wooded Landscape, with a mill stream to the left, and two figures in a boat angling.

## D. MYTENS, SEN.

47 Charles I. when a Child. He is represented at full length, in a green velvet dress with lace collar and ruffles, his right hand holds a small gun and his left rests on a sword, by his side a greyhound, behind him on a table a white hat ornamented with a feather and rich jewel clasp.

## G. DOUW.

48 A Young Girl at an arched window gathering a pink, a bird cage hangs above.

*Beautifully finished in all its details.*

## HANS HOLBEIN.

49 Portrait of the Princess Mary of England. She is represented in a standing position, draped in white, with a gold chain round her waist, the end of which sheholds in her hands. Painted on a green back ground.

*A rare and highly interesting portrait.*

## GASPAR NETSCHER.

50 Portrait of a Lady as Diana. A small whole length in a rich costume.

## D. TENIERS.

51 A Boor with a glass and mug.

## CLAUDE.

52 An Italian Landscape with distant scenery, and a bridge traversing the centre of the picture; to the right, in the foreground, two figures are in conversation under the shade of some trees; a flock of sheep and cattle are distributed over the landscape.

*A beautiful composition, full of effect and colour.*

30.

## ADRIAN OSTADE.

53 An Interior with four figures, the principal of whom, a woman, holds a book of music in her hand; to her left, a boor is tuning his violin; in the background are two men, one of whom has just filled his glass with beer.

## D. TENIERS.

54 Christ and the Woman of Samaria.
*A pasticcio in the manner of Titian.*

## WILLIAM MIERIS.

55 Portrait of the Artist in his Studio. *Brilliantly coloured.*

## JAN STEEN.

56 A Boor reading at a table.

## METZU.

57 An Interior with a cavalier singing, accompanied by a lady.

## C. POELÈMBURG.

58 The Glorification of the Virgin.
*An elegant composition, and brilliantly coloured.*

## DE WITTE.

59 The Annunciation to the Shepherds.

## PELLEGRINI DA MODENA.

60 The Virgin and Infant Saviour surrounded by Angels and Saints, a brilliant landscape is seen at the back.
*From the Collection of Lady Hampden.*

## P. BREUGHEL.

61 St. John Preaching—a composition of numerous figures, very minutely wrought

## RAFFAELLE.

62 The Flagellation—a composition of three figures; in the centre the Saviour tied to a pillar is receiving the lashes; the background of the picture is formed by a building with three arches, through which a landscape is seen.
*Formerly in the Collection of A. Hope, Esq.*

## BASSANO.

63 The Nativity. £12.

## MOUCHERON AND LINGELBACK.

64 An extensive Landscape with numerous figures, horses, dogs, &c. dispersed in groups over the picture, preparing to start for the chase.

## VAN BERGHEN.

65 A Landscape with a group of cattle and figures in the foreground, and a woman milking.

## RAFFAELLE.

66 The Virgin, Child and St. John in a landscape—small circular.

A replica of the picture known as La Vierge de la Maison d'Albe.

In a satin-wood case, enriched with twelve Wedgwood medallions.

## SIR B. WEST, P.R.A.

67 Renaldo and Amida.—The enchantress is here represented sitting, supporting the head of her lover, who is recumbent, holding his shield that serves for a mirror, to which her attention is invited by a cupid while arranging her hair. Behind is another cupid, gathering flowers, and three more at his feet. This is a production of the artist's best period.

*Signed and dated* 1766. *Retouched* 1790.

## J. VAN HAAGEN.

68 A View at the entrance of a Wood, with figures preparing for the chase.

*The effect of light and shade is beautifully rendered.*

## P. BRILL AND CARACCI.

69 A Landscape, with St. Francis kneeling and contemplating the Crucifix.

## GHIRLANDAJO (SCHOOL OF).

70 A Landscape, with the Virgin and Child attended by an Angel.

## PATEL.

71 A Landscape, with buildings and figures, and cattle in the foreground.

## DOMENICHINO.

72 A classical Landscape, with figures towing a boat.

## VANDYCK.

73 Christ Mocked. *A vigorous sketch.*

## BERKHEYDEN.

74 The Town Hall at Haarlem, with numerous figures.

## FRANCESCO MOLA.

75 The Repose of the Holy Family.

## CAMUCCINI.

76 The Virgin, Child, and St. John.

## A. CARACCI.

77 St. John Baptising the Saviour in the River Jordan.

## CANALETTO.

78 View of St. Mark's Place, with figures

## P. DA CORTONA.

79 The Holy Family in a Landscape, with Angels ministering.

## CANALETTO.

80 The Grand Canal, Venice, with numerous gondolas and figures.

## PREUDHOME, (of Neufchatel).

81 Portraits of The Duke of Hamilton, Doctor, and Sir John Moore.

## MAES.

82 William 1st Prince of Orange, a full length portrait in armour.

## MARTIN SCHOEN.

83 A Triptique, representing the Crucifixion, Christ leaving the Judgment Hall, and the Taking down from the Cross.

*An important and finely preserved work of this rare master.*

In a mahogany case, the outer door enriched with figures of Saints en grisaille.

## STELLA.

84 The Virgin and Child enthroned, with Saints worshipping.

## A DEL SARTO.

85 A Portrait of a Man in a black cap and dress, supposed to be the portrait of the Artist.

## TITIAN.

86 The Virgin and Child and St. John.

## CARLO MARATTI.

87 The Holy Family.

## ELSHEIMER.

88 The Holy Family in the Desert.

## HOLBEIN (SCHOOL).

89 Portrait of Martin Luther.

## L. DA VINCI.

90 A Portrait of La Joconda.

## ALONZO CANO.

91 The Vision of a Saint.

## FRANCIA.

92 The Virgin contemplating the Infant Saviour.

## F. GUARDI.

93 A Venetian scene, with figures.

## BERNADINO LUINI.

94 Artemesia holding the Vase containing the Ashes of her Husband.

*Exquisitely finished.*

## HOLBEIN.

95 A small full length Portrait of Edward the sixth, in a rich costume.

## RAFFAELLE (SCHOOL).

96 The Vision of Ezekiel.

*Originally in the Royal Collection at Madrid, and presented by Charles the fourth to the Duke of Lucca, of whom it was purchased by Lord Northwick.*

C. MARATTI.

97 The Holy Family.

G. BELLINI.

98 Portrait of a Lady in a green dress.

SCHIDONE.

99 The Holy Family,—oval

PRIMATICCIO.

100 Clelia with her companion Virgins, escaping from the camp of Porsenna.

*An important work by this rare master, engraved by Bonasone.*

*From the collection of Mr. Jennings the Antiquarian.*

TITIAN.

101 Venus reclining.

LUCAS KRANACK.

102 Cupid stung by Bees, making his lament to Venus. From the Odes of Anacreon. *Engraved.*

TITIAN (SCHOOL).

103 Venus, a sketch,—small.

TITIAN (SCHOOL).

104 Venus rising from the Sea.

CORREGGIO (SCHOOL).

105 Venus and Satyr.

*End of the First Day's Sale.*

# SECOND DAY'S SALE.

On WEDNESDAY, the 27th day of JULY, 1859,

AT ONE O'CLOCK PRECISELY.

LOT

## JAQUES CALLOT.

106 The Little Fair, with numerous figures. *The engraved picture.*

## MOUCHERON.

107 An upright Landscape, with figures.

## P. KOBEL.

108 Two Cows in a Landscape.

## E. VERBOECKHOVEN.

109 A Donkey and Sheep in a Stable.

## LINGLEBACK.

110 The departure for the Chase, with numerous horses and figures. *A work of great delicacy and tenderness of touch.*

## P. POTTER.

111 A Landscape, with a white horse, with a red cloak thrown over it, near it a dog and a man sleeping under a ruin.

*From Strawberry Hill.*

## RAFFAELLE.

112 Portrait of La Fornarina.

## D. TENIERS.

113 A Landscape, with the Artist and his Wife seated in the foreground.

## N. BERGHEM.

114 A Landscape, with two figures, seated near some rocks, and four cows variously grouped.

*Painted with great effect and truth to nature.*

## C. CIGNANI.

115 St. Francis in an attitude of devotion.

## CORNELIS.

116 Portrait of a Lady.

## ALBERT DURER (SCHOOL).

117 Portrait of a Nun at devotion.

## ZUCCHERO.

118 Portrait of Queen Elizabeth in a black dress, with a chain of pearls round her neck.

## A. CARACCI.

119 Polyphemus and the Sea Nymphs.

## SIR ANTHONY MORE.

120 Portrait of Queen Mary.

## PAUL VERONESE.

121 Portrait of Cosmo di Medicis, the founder of that Illustrious family.

## W VANDE VELDE.

122 Admiral Van Tromp. *Painted with great force and truth.* In the background a Sea Fight.

## DOBSON.

123 Sir William Farmor, groom of the Bedchamber to Charles Prince of Wales, in armour.

## ZUCCHERO.

124 Mary Queen of Scots, she holds in her hand three roses, and is habited in a rich costume, three quarter length.

## RIGAUD.

125 Phillippe d'Orleans, the Regent, in Armour, three quarter length.

VANDYCK.

126 Philip Herbert, Earl of Pembroke, Lord Chamberlain of the King's household, and Chancellor of the University of Oxford.

TITIAN,.

127 The Duke of Alva in armour.

HANS SCHAUFLEIN.

128 Portrait of a Mañ in a black robe,

P. BORDONE.

129 Portrait of a Lady.

PORBUS.

130 Portrait of the Emperor Charles fifth, in a rich dress, with the chain and order of the Golden Fleece.

PAUL VANSOMER.

131 The Earl of Arundel. A magnificent full length portrait of one of the earliest and most enthusiastic patrons of the fine arts; he is habited in black, and wears the garter; in the background a view of the house and gardens of Arundel Castle.

PAUL VANSOMER.

132 The Countess of Arundel. Companion to the preceding picture.

BOTTICELLI.

133 The Virgin and Child with Angels; circular.

AMBERGER.

134 Portrait of a Man in a black cap and dress.

AMBERGER.

135 Portrait of a Female in the dress of a Nun, landscape background. Companion to the preceding.

PAUL VANSOMER.

136 Lord de Lisle in his robes of state; a fine whole length portrait.

MARK GERRARD.

137 Portraits of the Earl of Dorset and his Secretary. The Earl is represented standing erect, preparing to receive a communication from his secretary, who holds in his right hand a letter addressed to his lordship, and in the other a petition from the Merchant Adventurers. *Admirably painted.*

# DINING ROOM.

## QUINTIN MATSYS.

138 The Artist painting his Mother's Portrait.

*A highly interesting work, painted with that power and truth to nature for which this master is so justly celebrated.*

## EARLY GREEK (SCHOOL).

139 The Death of St. Ephraim. *In a fine state of preservation.*

## VANDER GOES.

140 The Meeting of Joachim and Anna.

"On a certain feast day Joachim brought double offerings to the Lord, but the high priest, Isaachas, refused, saying—It is not lawful seeing that thou hast no issue in Israel; and Joachim was exceeding sorrowful, and would not be seen by his wife, but went into the pastures to the shepherds, and fasted forty days and nights. His wife, Anna, remained in her house, praying. And behold an Angel said to her, Anna, thy prayer is heard, see thy husband, Joachim is coming; for an Angel had spoken to him also: and they met at the Golden Gate, and Anna embraced her husband, saying—I, who was barren, shall become a joyful mother!"—*See Mrs. Jameson's Legends of Madonna.*

## BALDASSARE PERUZZI.

141 The Adoration of the Magi. A rocky Landscape, in the foreground of which the Virgin is seated, with the infant Jesus and Joseph, receiving the offerings of the Magi, who are surrounded by numerous attendants.

*A well preserved example of this rare master.*

## MAZZOLINO DI FERRARA.

142 Christ in the Judgment Hall. The principal subject represents the Saviour being conducted by Pilate down a flight of steps from the Upper into the Lower Judgment Hall, where several of the priests are seen exciting the populace to demand the condemnation of their prisoner.

*An admirable and highly-finished production of art, elaborate in its composition, and varied in its details. From the collection of Allan Gilmore, Esq.*

## HOBBIMA.

143 A grand Landscape, with a winding road runing through the centre of the picture, along which several figures are travelling, and others are halting at the door of an Inn; to the left, a cavalier with huntsman and dogs is pursuing the chase.

## LOCATELLI.

144 An Italian Landscape with figures. A classical composition, embracing great extent and variety of scenery; a group of four figures is placed on an eminence on the left of the picture; to the right, a herd of cattle, driven by peasants, and in the foreground, a man urging a dog.

*The colouring is very pleasing and excellent throughout.*

## MORONI.

145 Alessandro Farnese, Prince of Parma. He is represented in three quarter length, dressed in an elaborate suit of armour, and holds in one hand a letter and in the other a baton. A very fine portrait; the details, especially the armour, are finished in the most masterly manner.

## BASSANO.

146 Portraits of Jacobus Mauroc and his Son.

## TINTORETTO.

147 A Doge of Venice. He is represented seated, in the rich costume of his office. *Full of dignity and expression.*

## GERMAN (SCHOOL).

148 Portrait of a Gentleman in a black dress and hat, holding a scroll in one hand.

## GIORGIONE.

149 Gaston de Foix in armour, with a hat and feathers.

*From the Lucca Gallery.*

## TITIAN.

150 The Emperor Vitellius.

Believed to be one of the Twelve Cæsars, painted for Gonzaga, Duke of Mantua, whose entire collection was purchased by Charles the First, but sold again by the Commonwealth and dispersed. It is a fine colossal figure.

TITIAN.

151 The Emperor Vespasian—Companion to the preceding. From the same collection

REMBRANDT (AFTER).

152 A three-quarter Portrait of a Gentleman, in a black dress and hat, with a lace collar, in one hand he holds a glove.

REMBRANDT (AFTER).

153 Portrait of a Lady holding a fan; companion to the preceding.

P. REINAGLE.

154 The Sermon, from Tristam Shandy.

The characters introduced are Mr. Shandy, Uncle Toby, Dr. Slop, and Corporal Trim. Those who recollect the passage which it illustrates, will at once detect its graphic and forcible delineation.

LE NAIN.

155 Interior of a Peasant's Cottage with figures.

*Painted with great breadth and truth.*

J. B. WEENIX.

156 A View in the Garden of a Château; in the foreground, a finely sculptured fountain, on the pedestal of which is grouped a rich assemblage of fruits and flowers, and in the midst a monkey, whose enjoyment is disturbed by the sudden appearance of a hawk; to the right, in the foreground, a fine peacock displays the beauty of its plumage. *A very important work.*

TITIAN.

157 Portrait of Pope Paul IV.

HOGARTH.

158 The Modern Midnight Conversation.

TINTORETTO.

159 Portrait of Doge Venieri, who commanded at the Battle of Lepanto.

N. MAAS.

160 Vertumnus and Pomona.

*A fine work of this admired master.*

## BASSANO.

161 The Family Concert—A group of ten figures, being portraits of the Ponte and Bassano Family.

## S. DEL PIOMBO.

162 Portrait of a Lady in a black dress.

## TITIAN.

163 Head of a Doge of Venice

## BERNARD VAN ORLAY.

164 Portrait of a Duchess of Burgundy; she is dressed in the richly jewelled costume of the period, and wears a hat and feathers

## JOHN DE MABUSE.

165 St. Veronica exhibiting to St. Peter and St. Paul the Handkerchief which had received the Impression of the Saviour's countenance.

## GUIDO.

166 Portrait, life size, of Cardinal Barbarini, seated in a chair

## SIR ANTHONY MORE.

167 Charles Brandon Duke of Suffolk, Lord Great Master to King Henry VIII. He is represented in a black velvet dress, trimmed with fur, and a cap with a white feather, holding the hilt of his sword in his left hand, the right resting on a pillar.
*A rare and beautiful portrait.*

## BRONZINO.

168 Portrait of the Duchess of Parma, in a black dress, covered with jewels, in her right hand she holds a fan.

## ANTONIO CANALETTO.

170 The Grand Canal at Venice—A Scene during the Gala della Spolializza, animated by fancifully decorated Gondolas and numerous figures of every description. *An important work.*

## VANDYKE.

171 Antonio Trieste, Bishop of Ghent. He is represented seated in a chair, holding a letter in his right hand.
*A very fine portrait, painted with great force and vigour.*

## VAN EYCK.

172 The Adoration of the Magi. Under the Porch of an extensive Gothic building, through which a distant landscape is seen, the Virgin is seated with the Infant in her lap, attended by Joseph. Two of the Magi are kneeling before her, presenting their gifts, the third is approaching; behind him are the attendants of the Magi and a dog.

*An important work of this rare master, in a beautiful state of preservation.*

## MARTIN SCHOEN.

173 Christ bearing his Cross, and St. Veronica.

*From the collection of the Archbishop of Mayence. Engrvaed.*

## ANGELICA DA FIESOLE.

174 The Legend of St. Cosmo and St. Damian.

## ALBANO.

175 The Creation—The Lord conversing with Adam and Eve; arched top

## ANTONILEZ.

176 Portrait of a Man, in a red cap and black dress.

## GERMAN (SCHOOL).

177 Henry the Holy, of Bavaria, at his devotions.

## LUCA SIGNORELLI.

178 Four Figures of Saints.

## MORONI.

179 A Portrait—one of the Medici Family.

## N. POUSSIN.

180 The Triumph of Flora.

## JANET.

181 Portrait of the Duc de Guise.

## TITIAN.

182 "Danæ." *From the collection of Prince Belvedere of Naples.*

## IN CORRIDOR AND BED ROOMS.

CANALETTO (SCHOOL).

183 A pair—Scenes on the Grand Canal, Venice.

TIMOTEO DELLA VITE.

184 The Virgin and Child.

RAFFAELLE (AFTER).

185 The Holy Family.

WOHLGEMUTH.

186 Christ bearing his Cross.

P. VERONESE.

187 The Coronation of the Virgin. *A sketch.*

GIORGIONE.

188 The Holy Family in a landscape.

WOHLGEMUTH.

189 The Crucifixion.

ANGELICA KAUFFMAN.

190 The Departure of Hagar.

BONINGTON (AFTER).

191 The Doge's Palace, Venice.

CORREGGIO (SCHOOL).

192 The Holy Family.

TIMOTEO DELLA VITE.

193 Dead Christ supported by Angels.

FRANCIA.

194 Holy Family.

A. KAUFFMAN.

195 The Artist's Portrait.

PERUGINO.

196 The Virgin and Child.

GIORGIONE.

197 Virgin and Child with Saints.

A DEL SARTO.

198 Holy Family.

ZUCCHERELLI.

199 Landscape and figures.

HILTON.

200 A View in Northwick Park.

SIR G. KNELLER.

201 Portrait of George I. in his royal robes.

GILPIN.

202 A Landscape with figures and horses.

A. CARACCI.

203 The Triumph of Bacchus.

204 Six large engravings, after Le Brun, representing the Triumphs of Alexander the Great; *framed and varnished.*

*End of the Second Day's Sale.*

# THIRD DAY'S SALE.

On THURSDAY, the 28th day of JULY, 1859,

AT ONE O'CLOCK PRECISELY.

## BED ROOMS.

S. ROSA.

205 A Rocky Scene with figures.

J. ROMANO.

206 The Graces; *on two panels.*

C. STELLA.

207 The Adoration of the Shepherds.

A. CARACCI.

208 An Italian Landscape with figures.

TIEPOLO.

209 Saint Carlo Borromeo at the Hospital Gate.

SPANISH (SCHOOL).

210 Mother and Child.

VANDYCK.

211 Samson being bound.

J. ROMANO.

212 Mount Parnassus.

## S. RUYSDAEL.

213 A River Scene with boats and figures.

## L. GIORDANO.

214 The Adoration of the Shepherds.

## PULIGO.

215 The Virgin and Child and Joseph in a landscape.

## ALONZO CANO.

216 Joseph and the Virgin leading the Infant Jesus.

## ECKHOUT.

217 Portrait of a Man in a black dress.

## SCHOOL OF PERUGINO.

218 The Virgin and Child.

## DOMENICHINO.

219 A Landscape and figures.

## L. VAN LEYDEN.

220 The Virgin and Child.

## TINTORETTO.

221 Portrait of a Gentleman in black.

## DA VINCI (SCHOOL).

222 The Holy Family in a rocky landscape.

## MUZIANO.

223 The Coronation of the Virgin.

## PULIGO.

224 The Adoration of the Infant Saviour.

# THE CABINET ROOM.

## SCHIAVONE.

225 The Death of Adonis.

*A grand composition; the figures well drawn and finely coloured.*

## DOBSON.

226 Portrait of the Earl of Carnarvon.

## SIR P. LELY.

227 Portrait of Sir W. Godolphin.

## GUERCINO.

228 Il Condottiere. A spirited half length of a warrior in complete armour with uplifted sword, said to be intended for one of the leaders of the "Free Companies" or "Lances," whose achievements occupied so prominent a place in the history of the Italian States during the Middle Ages. Above, on the left, is the inscription, "*Spirans Minarum et Cædes.*"

*It is brilliantly coloured. From the collection of Sir S. Clarke.*

## F. QUELLINUS.

229 Artemesia drinking her Husband's Ashes.

## VANDYCK.

230 Portrait of the Earl of Strafford, three-quarter length.

*Full of dignity and expression.*

## GUIDO.

231 Cupid reposing in a landscape.

## HOGARTH

232 Dr. Locke, Founder of the Locke Hospital. A portrait of the celebrated Architect of the Locke Hospital, a plan of which he holds in his hand.

*It came into possession of its noble owner from the collection of Sir John Thorold.*

RUBENS.

233 Portrait of Mdlle. Lundens.

PARMEGIANO.

234 Cosmo di Medicis.
*A fine portrait, painted on a green background,*

A. CUYP.

235 A Landscape, with a youth holding the reins of three horses, one a dappled gray; near him, a dog; some buildings are seen in the distance.

KAREL DU JARDIN.

236 An upright Landscape, a white horse laden with a pack, and a man conversing with a female.

TITIAN.

237 Portrait of Luigi Cornaro.

ADRIAN VAN DE VELDE.

238 A Landscape; in the foreground, a dun cow about to drink at a pool; further on, another and two sheep are lying down; in the distance, a third is grazing; to the left, on a hillock, are some farm buildings.

PAUL POTTER.

239 The Exterior of a Farm; in the foreground are four cows, two of which are lying down; to the left, a milkmaid with her pails; and in the background, a river with two men in a boat.

RAFFAELLE.

240 A Landscape, with the Martyrdom of Saint Sebastian—a composition of ten figures.

DE LORME AND LINGLEBACK.

241 Interior of a Church in Holland, with figures variously grouped.

S. ROSA.

242 A Rocky Landscape with figures.

JACOB RUYSDAEL.

243 A Mountainous Landscape, with a cascade of water falling over the rocks in the foreground.

## VAN STRY.

244 A Landscape, with a peasant driving cattle to water. 11

## W. VAN DE VELDE.

245 A Marine View, with English men-of-war.

## G. CUYP.

246 A Landscape with cavaliers, huntsmen and dogs preparing for the chase.

## WYNANTS.

247 A Landscape, with figures preparing for hawking.

## F. MILLET.

248 A Classical Landscape with figures—effect of storm.

## S. ROSA.

249 A Landscape, Scene on the Coast of the Bay of Salerno; three figures are grouped on a rock in the foreground.

## J. VAN HUYSUM.

250 The Artist's Portrait; he is holding in his right hand a palette, and in his left an unfinished picture.

*A rare and interesting portrait.*

## BRONZINO.

251 Portrait of a Child in a red dress, seated on a cushion, playing with a dog; supposed to be one of the family of Cosmo di Medicis.

## VANDYCK.

252 Portrait of the Princess Mary, daughter of Charles I.

*From the collection of Lord Cowley; oval.*

... ... ...

253 Portrait of Lady Jane Seymour.

## ANGELICA KAUFFMAN.

254 Cupid drawn by the Graces; *circular.*

## ANGELICA KAUFFMAN.

255 Cupid disarmed by the Graces—companion to the preceding. 12

GUIDO (AFTER).

256 Fortune scattering her Favours over the Earth.

VANDER CAPELLA.

257 A Marine View—a Calm; to the right of the picture is a jetty, on both sides of which several yachts and boats are at anchor; in front, a boat containing a party of ladies and gentlemen about to land; in the offing are four men-of-war, one of which is firing a salute.

*A capital work of the master. From the Lapeyrière collection.*

VELASQUEZ.

258 The Four Philosophers—a copy, by Velasquez, of the famous picture in the Pitti Palace, by Rubens, and containing portraits of Velasquez himself, Rubens, Lypsius and Grotius.

*It was brought into England by the Duke de San Carlos, from the collection of the Marquis Urquijo, of Madrid.*

FRANCESCO MOLA.

259 The Sybil.

GUIDO.

260 Cupid rifling the Casket.

GERMAN (SCHOOL).

261 Portrait of a Man with a book in his hand, probably one of the Reformers.

MURILLO.

262 Portrait of Francisco de Quevedo de Villegas, the celebrated author

GIORGIONE.

263 Portrait of Angelus Politianus.

VANDER HELST.

264 Portrait of General David Leslie, a Distinguished Officer in the time of Charles.

W. VAN DE VELDE.

265 A Calm, with vessels and boats at anchor.

*Exhibited in the British Institution in 1837.*

## QUINTIN MATSYS.

266 Portrait of a Youth in a black cap, reading a letter.

*An admirable work by this rare master.*

## SIR A. MORE.

267 Portrait of Lord William Russell when a youth.

## REINAGLE.

268 A Rocky Landscape, with a wooden bridge and cattle in the foreground.

## RUBENS.

269 A Landscape, with figures representing Philip's Interview with the Eunuch

## P. BRILL AND A. CARACCI.

270 A Landscape with figures departing for the chase.

## W. VAN DE VELDE.

271 A Marine View, with men-of-war and boats at anchor.

## ALBERT CUYP.

272 A warm sunny Landscape, with distant View of the town of Dort; in the foreground, a group of four cows, and a boy and dog asleep.

## JAN MIEL.

273 A Mountainous Landscape, with a rocky path and figures.

## LUCAS VAN LEYDEN.

274 The Meeting of David and Abigail.

*A curious old painting, especially interesting as exhibiting the state of art at the time of its production. Its subject will be found narrated in the 25th chapter of Sam.* 1.

## NICHOLAS BERGHEM.

275 Rural Felicity—a Grand Landscape, with shepherds and shepherdesses disporting, surrounded by their flocks.

*A fine work, painted in* 1647 *for the Burgomaster Vanderhulk of Dort. Engraved.*

## BASSANO.

276 The Annunciation to the Shepherds.

## JAN WILLS.

277 A Landscape with a group of figures and cattle in the foreground.

## GONZALES COQUES.

278 Family Portraits. *From the Saltmarshe Gallery.*

## BOTH.

279 A Landscape with figures. In the upper part of the picture, cattle and figures are seen crossing a stream, just above a waterfall; and in the left foreground are a man and woman proceeding in an opposite direction.

## TITIAN.

280 St. Jerome praying in a landscape.

## ALBANO.

281 Sleeping Cupids disarmed by Nymphs in a landscape.
*From the collection of Sir Simon Clarke.*

## W. VAN DE VELDE.

282 A Sea Piece with vessels—a fresh Breeze.
*Exhibited at the British Institution in* 1837.

## JAN STEEN.

283 A Dutch Fair; a busy, bustling Scene, and cleverly treated. The house in the right-hand corner of the picture is said to be a view of Jan Steen's favourite cabaret, and in one of the rooms in which many of his choicest paintings were executed.

## D. CRESPI.

284 A Landscape with cupids and nymphs asleep.

## JACOB RUYSDAEL.

285 A richly composed Landscape, with wooded scenery to the right; in the foreground, a cascade of water, and in the distance figures and cattle.

ADRIAN VAN DE VELDE.

286 An Italian Landscape, with a herdsman driving a flock of cattle and sheep through a stream.

GONZALES COQUES.

287 A group of Family Portraits.
*Very highly finished.*

CLAUDE.

288 A richly diversified Landscape, with a lake in the distance, and a castle on an eminence; in the foreground, three cows and a peasant.

WALKER.

289 Small Portrait of Secretary Thurlow.

WALKER.

290 Oliver Cromwell in armour.

C. DE BAAN.

291 Portrait of a Nobleman; small.

STOTHARD.

292 The Arts and Sciences.

## ENTRANCE HALL.

BOTTICELLI (SCHOOL).

293 The Holy Family; *circular.*

A. KAUFFMAN.

294 A pair—Mythological Subjects; *circular*

A. KAUFFMAN.

295 Another pair.

L. PENNI.

296 The Holy Family.

### HOFLAND.

297 View in Northwick Park, with cows in the foreground.

### HOFLAND.

298 View of Northwick House, with the lake and deer in the foreground.

### DEL SARTO (SCHOOL).

299 The Holy Family.

### GLOVER.

300 View of Harrow-on-the-Hill.

### GLOVER.

301 Harrow Park and Grounds.

### FRA BARTOLOMEO.

302 The Holy Family; *circular.*

### RAFFAELLE (SCHOOL).

303 The Virgin and Child with attendant angels.

### PARMEGIANO (SCHOOL).

304 The Virgin and Child and St. John.

### PLATZER.

305 Coronation of Bacchus. *A capital example of the master.*

*End of the Third Day's Sale.*

# FOURTH DAY'S SALE.

On FRIDAY, the 29th day of JULY, 1859,

AT ONE O'CLOCK PRECISELY.

## MODERN PICTURES.

### THE LIBRARY.

LOT

J. LEWIS.

306 Lion and Lioness—a sketch.

MONTAGUE.

307 The Village Churchyard.

DUVAL.

308 A View on the Downs, with shepherd and sheep.

UWINS.

309 The Gulf of Spezzia, Castle of Tereci in the distance.

H. P. PARKER.

310 Northumberland Fisher Girl.

PETHER.

311 Cheyne Walk, Chelsea, by moonlight.

STOTHARD.

312 A Group of Figures dancing.

OVERLAET.

313 The Chapeau de Paille, after RUBENS. *A fine drawing.*

## G. A. WILLIAMS.

314 View of Medmenham Abbey.

## J. WILSON.

315 A Coast Scene, sunset.

## SIR C. EASTLAKE, P.R.A.

316 View of the Erectheum.

## COBBETT.

317 Market Girls on the French Coast.

## T. WOODWARD.

318 Scotch Lassie tending Cattle.

## E. W. COOKE.

319 Ruins of Martello Tower at Capo Dorso.

## ZEITTER.

320 Hungarians at the Shrine.

## J. C. HOOK.

321 "A Dream of Venice." Figures in a gondola, and a young lady bending down from a balcony presenting a rose to a cavalier.

*Exhibited at the Exhibition in Paris.*

## SIR J. REYNOLDS.

322 The Infant Hercules.

*A sketch for the picture painted for the Empress Catherine of Russia.*

## J. BODDINGTON.

323 The Sequestered Glen.

## SIDNEY PERCY.

324 Woodland Pasture.

## LINTON.

325 View of Lord Northwick's Grounds at Harrow.

### J. BONINGTON.

326 A Sea Beach, with boys and fish. *Painted in the artist's best time.*

### COPLEY FIELDING.

327 The old Groyne at Brighton. *Very spirited and effective.*

### FROST, A.R.A.

328 Sabrina. *A charming work.*

### W. SHAYER.

329 A Coast Scene, with figures and boats.

### F. LEE, R.A.

330 A View of the Mansion and grounds, Northwick Park.

### W. MÜLLER.

331 A Landscape, with bivouac of gypsies.

### STARK.

332 A Wooded Glen.

### SIR J. REYNOLDS.

333 The Infant St. John with the Lamb.

### PETHER.

334 A Landscape, with the ruins of a temple and river scenery—moonlight.

### COBBETT.

335 View of the Lake in Northwick Park.

### EDMONSTONE.

336 The Young Showman.

### REINAGLE.

337 A Landscape, with a waterfall.

### WOOLMER.

338 Fitz Eustace—a scene from Marmion.

### MORTON.

339 An Indian holding a Goblet.

BELL SMITH.

340 The Visit to the Spring.

DENIS.

341 The Falls of Tivoli.

DENIS.

342 Ruins of the Temple of Minerva—companion to the preceding.

MÜLLER.

343 A Winter Landscape, with Sportsman and Dog.

H. GRITTEN.

344 Oberwesel on the Rhine, and the Castle of Schonberg.

H. JUTSUM.

345 A Westmorland Trout Stream.

SCOTT.

346 Battersea Bridge and the Old Swan Tavern, with figures.

J. ECKFORD LAUDER.

347 The Maiden's Reverie. *A charming work.*

A. GILBERT.

348 A Wooded Scene in Sussex, with felled timber and figures—approaching storm.

VIREY.

349 A Moonlight Scene.

SIR C. EASTLAKE, P.R.A.

350 A Peasant Girl of Albano leading her Blind Mother to Mass.

PATRICK NASMYTH.

351 View in Leigh Woods, with a bivouac of gypsies.

*An important and highly finished work of this admired artist. Painted for Lord Northwick.*

OLD CROME.

352 A Landscape, with a clump of trees and cows in the foreground.

JULIETTE BONHEUR.

353 A Group of Turkeys in a Landscape.

A. GILBERT.

354 A River Scene—sunrise. *Poetically treated.*

SIR J. REYNOLDS.

355 Portrait of an Officer.

NASH.

356 Portia and her Suitors—from the Merchant of Venice.

H. BARRAUD.

357 An Incident in the late Crimean War—Balacklava.

PALADINI (AFTER RAFFAELLE).

358 The Holy Family.

## PARLOUR.

W. POOL.

359 Beggar Boy thinking of the Future. *A work of great merit.*

F. LEE, R.A.

360 View of Northwick Park and Mansion, with the lake in the foreground, and herd of deer swimming across.

J. WARD, R.A.

361 The Battle of Marston Moor. The figures, both of men and horses, are admirably grouped; in the foreground is a soldier presenting to Cromwell the helmet which had fallen from his head in the melèe of the fierce struggle there represented; while in the distance is shown the charge on the royal cavalry, which, as well as the other movements of the field, are very spirited.

*The colouring is excellent throughout.*

DOUGLAS COWPER.

362 A Scene from the Merchant of Venice.

## PATRICK NASMYTH.

363 A Scene near Harrow.

## SCHOTEL.

364 A Sea View, boats in a stiff breeze; the light and buoyant clouds give effect to the scene.

## WOOLMER.

365 Lucy Ashton.

## JOSEPH VERNET.

366 A Rocky Coast Scene, with wrecked vessels and figures in the foreground.

## W. MÜLLER.

367 A Canal Scene, Venice—a sketch.

## KREMER.

368 The Parting Glass. The principle figure is said to be intended for Brauwer, taking leave of his sweetheart.

*The picture is admirably painted.*

## G. MORLAND.

369 A Landscape, with two shepherds and their dogs.

*Painted with great freedom.*

## J. LINNELL, Sen.

370 A Landscape, with a winding road bordered by trees, and a flock of sheep passing along; in the foreground, a group of six cows at a pool, tended by a boy, and to the left, two figures and a child seated on a hillock. *Painted in 1849.*

## SIR THOMAS LAWRENCE.

371 Portrait of the Right Hon. William Pitt; three quarter length, in a standing position. *The celebrated picture.*

## JACOBS.

372 A View on the Coast of Greece.

## F. LEE, R.A.

373 View at Redleaf, near Penshurst, Sussex.

*A fine example of the master.*

### T. S. COOPER, A.R.A.

374 A Scene in Canterbury Meadows, with cattle grazing in the distance; in the forground, a black bull, and two cows reposing.
*Admirably grouped and finished. Painted in 1849.*

### SIR AUGUSTUS CALCOTT.

375 A Mill Pond, with Water Wheel; in the foreground, a man fishing.
*This fine picture may be regarded as one of the artist's most successful efforts.*

### WOOLMER.

376 Parisina.

### MODERN.

377 A Child with a Basket of Flowers on her arm.

### E. W. COOKE, R.A.

378 Scheveling Sands—Low Water.
*An excellent picture, the boats on the beach, and the groups of peasants and fishermen, painted with great freedom and spirit.*

### T. WEBSTER, R.A.

379 The Breakfast, or the Dunce Punished.
*The celebrated picture. Painted in 1838 for Lord Northwick. Not engraved.*

### A. MORTON.

380 A Scene at Apsley House.—The Duke of Wellington explaining to Colonel Gurwood, (the compiler of his dispatches), the date of that which gives the details of the Battle of Waterloo.

### G. E. HERRING.

381 View of the Gulf of Spezzia.

### ANGELICA KAUFFMAN.

382 The Graces decorating the bust of Handel.

### T. S. COOPER, A.R.A.

383 A Landscape, with a group of five cows reposing.
*A small but beautiful picture, painted in a clear and brilliant tone.*

### HOPPNER.

384 A little Girl, with a bunch of wild flowers.

## E. W. COOKE, R.A.

385 Scheveling Sands—a fresh breeze, a fishing smack getting off the shore. Companion to lot 378.

## W. MULREADY, R.A.

386 The Convalescent from Waterloo.
*The celebrated picture. Painted for Lord Northwick.*

## W. COLLINS, R.A.

387 An Old Roman Peasant.

## H. GRITTEN.

388 Interior of the Church of Caudebec.

*End of Fourth Day's Sale.* abme £ 7000

# FIFTH DAY'S SALE.

On TUESDAY, the 2nd day of AUGUST, 1859,

AT ONE O'CLOCK PRECISELY.

## THE LANDSCAPE ROOM.

LOT

FILIPPO LAURI.

390 Venus asleep—surprised by two satyrs.

FILIPPO LAURI.

391 The Power of Love—companion.

PORBUS.

392 Marie de Medicis.

ALBANO.

393 Three Females, representing Earth, Air and Water.

VALENTINO.

394 A Man Singing. *Very bold and effective.*

G. PENNI.

395 The Artist's Portrait, in a black dress and cap; green background

VALENTINO.

396 Two Angel's Heads. *Finely painted.*

L. DE HEERE.

397 Robert Devereux, Earl of Essex.

## SOLOMON RUYSDAEL.

398 A Landscape with a river and wood scenery, and men in a boat fishing.

## VANDYKE.

399 Justus Souterman.

*A fine portrait, painted with great freedom.*

## MORTON.

400 Italian Beggar Boys, with monkeys, dogs, &c.

*The subject well told and the colouring effective.*

## HOLBEIN.

401 A highly interesting Portrait of Sir A. Browne, Master of the Horse and Standard Bearer to Henry VIII. He attended the King to the Field of the Cloth of Gold.

## VANDYKE.

402 William, Earl of Pembroke.

## GERARD HONTHORST.

403 Jesus bound, brought before Caiaphas.

## O. MARINARI.

404 Bust of a Youth in a crimson cap and feather.

## JAQUES JORDAENS.

405 Pan pursuing Syrinx.

*A composition of five figures, rich in tone and brilliantly coloured.*

## PAUL POTTER.

406 A Landscape with a group of four cows under a tree, one lying down; cattle and sheep grazing in the distance.

## SIR J. REYNOLDS.

407 Portrait of the Duke of Cumberland; he is represented nearly at full-length in his robes of state, with the collar of S.S. and the George. *An admirable portrait.*

## HOGARTH.

408 The Hazard Table. The diversity of expression, and the varied effects produced on the gestures and movements of the company assembled, by the last cast of the dice, are admirably depicted.

## NICOLO POUSSIN.

409 An Italian Landscape with a distant river, and two figures conversing in the foreground.

## ALBERT CUYP.

410 The Harvest Moon. In the foreground, on the right, a group of cattle, further back are reapers harvesting; behind these objects a church tower prominently presents itself, partly hidden by trees; to the left, a group of buildings, behind which is seen the rising moon, which gives effect to the landscape.

## P. DA CORTONA.

411 The Parting of Jacob and Laban.

## VELASQUEZ.

412 A Grand Landscape with a group of figures in a boat.

## SIR P. LELY.

413 Portrait of Mrs. Trevor.

## SPANISH SCHOOL.

414 Portrait of Clara Eugenia Isabella, daughter of Philip the Second of Spain.

## RAZZI.

415 The Countess Spenocchi and Children, represented as "Charity."

*A fine specimen of this rare master, who was the founder of the Siennese School.*

## CLAUDE LORRAINE.

416 A Poetical Landscape, with a river winding through a hilly country; to the left, a castellated building with an archway; and in the foreground, which is richly diversified with trees and shrubs, a herdsman is seated playing on a pipe; a flock of sheep and cattle are dispersed over the scene.

*A beautiful work of the master, and in a fine state of preservation. Signed Claudio Gillee ft.*

## CAMPHUYSEN.

417 View of a Dairy Farm in Holland. A landscape richly illumined by the setting sun, in the foreground of which two figures are examining an ox; to the right, a group of three cows, and further back, a lady and gentleman standing in front of a cottage; to the left, in the distance, are farm buildings, a ruin, and cows grazing, which give effect and interest to the scene.

*This fine work is regarded as the chef d'œuvre of the master. From the Solly collection.* £

## PRINS.

418 A Canal Scene, Holland, with numerous boats, figures, and buildings. *Minutely finished.*

## BOLOGNESE

419 A Sicilian Landscape, with figures.

## JAN STEEN.

420 Peasants Saying Grace.

## CLAUDE LORRAINE.

421 A Marine Landscape, with stately arches and edifices on the right; to the left, a large ship is at anchor, from which bales of mer. chandise are being landed; various figures are grouped over the scene; and in the foreground lie the ruins of columns, statues, &c.

*From the collection of Sir Drummond Smith. Smith's Catalogue, Supplement No. 2, page* 804.

## P. DE CHAMPAGNE.

422 Portrait of Count Molé, three quarter length, seated.

## TITIAN.

423 Portrait of a Lady, in a rich Venetian costume; supposed to be the Artist's Daughter.

## NICOLO POUSSIN.

424 The Lake of Bolsenna. In the foreground is a herdsman leaning on his staff, attending a herd of goats; and on the further side of the lake a shepherd driving his flock to water.

## GASPAR POUSSIN.

425 A romantic Landscape, with distant Mountains; in the foreground are two figures; and further on, a shepherd tending cattle, drinking at a stream.

*From the Strawberry Hill collection.*

## OMMEGANCK.

426 A Landscape, with a mountainous pass, through which, a peasant on a horse, and a female, are driving a flock of sheep, cows, and goats.

## CLAUDE LORRAINE.

427 A Landscape, evening; to the left, a water mill and a bridge, over which a peasant is passing; in the centre of the picture, a flock of cattle are being driven by a woman on a mule, followed by two men.

## TITIAN.

428 Portrait of a Venetian Nobleman.

## GELDORP.

429 Portrait of a Gentleman in a ruff, holding a roll of music in his hand.

## BRONZINO

430 Portrait of Michael Angelo.

## C. JANSEN.

431 Portrait of Fletcher, the Dramatist.

*Painted in an oval, signed Cornelius Johnson, fecit* 1626.

## DIEPENBECK.

432 A Lady with a Child asleep.

## S. DE KONINGH.

433 A Landscape with distant scenery; in the foreground, a winding road with a cavalier and an attendant hawk ing.

## WILLIAM VANDEVELDE.

434 The English Fleet putting out to Sea, preparatory to the Battle of Sole Bay.

## WILLIAM VANDEVELDE.

435 The Battle of Sole Bay; a spirited representation of the famous Naval Engagement which took place June 1st, 1665; in front the enemy's fire boat is seen in the act of striking the Admiral's ship.

*** This and the preceding picture were formerly in the possession of Lord Methuen, for whose ancestor they were painted.

## PAUL VANSOMER.

436 Henry, Prince of Wales, a fine full-length portrait.

## PAUL VANSOMER.

437 Elizabeth of Bohemia—companion picture to the preceding.

## CARLO MARATTI.

438 Diana and her Nymphs surprised by Acteon,

## CUYP.

439 A River View, with a group of cattle on its banks and a shepherd piping.

## GASPAR POUSSIN.

440 A grand Landscape, the background richly wooded, with mountains in the distance; in the foreground are two figures reposing.

## CLAUDE LORRAINE.

441 Apollo and the Cumæan Sibyl.

The view here represented is taken from the summit of a cliff, from whence the spectator views the upper parts of the once noble edifices of the city of Cumæ; looking from thence to a spacious bay of the sea, bounded on one side by mountains; on the left is seen the Temple of the Sibyllæ, built on the verge of a rock. In the foreground are the Sibyl of Cumæ and Apollo; the former is seated on a stone, apparently preferring her request to the god who stands before her. A cluster of shrubs and fragments of ancient buildings are scattered over the foreground, on which browse a number of goats.

## C. JANSEN.

442 Portrait of General Ireton—half length.

## HOPPNER.

434 A full-length Portrait of George the Fourth when Prince of Wales, in his robes of state.

## MORONI.

444 Portrait of a Nobleman in Armour and his Son.

## LUDOLPH BACKHUYSEN,

445 A View on the Texel Coast, during a fresh breeze. The composition of this excellent production represents a group of persons on a sandy shore in front, one of whom, an old sailor with a stick, is conversing with a man and two women, sitting on the ground, and behind him stands a boy. A boat with eight persons in it is seen approaching the shore; beyond this object is a sloop, with her sails furled. On the left are two fishing boats, close to some piles; a little remote from these is a ship of war, and still farther are two frigates.

*Smith's Catalogue, No.* 126, *page* 443.

## GASPAR POUSSIN.

446 A grand Landscape, richly diversified with buildings, trees, and mountains, and in the foreground two figures reposing—effect of evening.

## PAUL BRILL.

447 A Landscape, with the Virgin and Child seated, and angels bearing the cross, and other emblems of the Saviour's sufferings.

## CARLO CIGNANI.

448 The Holy Family.

## P. VERONESE.

449 Portrait of a Gentleman in a black dress.

## RUBENS.

450 The Princess of Orange, three-quarter length.

## ALBERT CUYP.

451 A Landscape, with two cows reposing near a rock, attended by a herdsman leaning on his staff; in the distance are three other figures, and the view is terminated by a river; a gleam of sunshine illumines the whole.

## NICHOLAS BERGHEM.

452 A grand Italian Landscape, with a team of four oxen drawing a cart laden with stone, driven by two peasants; in the foreground, a herdsman tending cattle and sheep. *Engraved.*

VANDYCK.

453 Portrait of the Archduke Ferdinand.

T. G. CUYP.

454 Portrait of the Wife of Albert Cuyp. *Signed and dated.*

PAUL POTTER.

455 A Landscape, with a group of two cows and a sheep reposing on a hillock, in the shade of a tree; a milk maid with her pails, completes the composition.

MURILLO.

456 Jacob placing the Peeled Rods before the Sheep of Laban.

The celebrated picture from the St Jago Palace at Madrid, where it formed one of the series originally executed for the Marquis of Villarmarque.

LOUIS DAVID.

457 Belisarius begging at the Gates of Carthage.

*An important work by that great French painter.*

## THE VENETIAN ROOM.

BACKHUYSEN.

458 The Artist's Portrait. He is pourtrayed in nearly a front view; in the background, a sea port.

BREUGHEL.

459 The Coronation of the Virgin, in a circle surrounded by flowers.

LINGLEBACK.

460 The Departure for the Chase. *A work of the highest quality.*

SIR F. BOURGEOIS.

461 A Shipwreck. *Painted with great spirit and effect.*

CANALETTO.

462 A Canal Scene.

CANALETTO.

463 A Canal Scene. The companion to the preceding.

GAINSBOROUGH.

464 The Tired Ploughman.

BONINGTON.

465 A Coast Scene, with figures and a timber waggon.

CANALETTO.

466 View on the Grand Canal—Venice.

CANALETTO.

467 View of the Dogana; companion.

GASPAR POUSSIN.

468 A grand Landscape, with the subject of Saint Hubert and the Stag.
*This magnificent work formerly adorned the Francavilla Palace at Rome.*

SMITH OF CHICHESTER.

469 A Landscape and figures.

HODGES.

470 View of part of Mount Pausilyppo, towards Naples.

JOSEPH VERNET.

471 An Italian Sea Port, with a lighthouse, and figures in the foreground pushing a boat off.

SIR J. REYNOLDS.

472 Sketch of the Head of one of the Female Figures by Raffaelle, in the Incendro del Borgo.
*From the collection of Sir T. Lawrence.*

WATTEAU.

473 The Return from the Chase.

WATTEAU.

474 The Lion Hunt; companion.

SIR J. REYNOLDS.

475 Portrait of the Hon. Mrs. Barrington. *Very elegant.*

JACOB RUYSDAEL.

476 An upright Landscape; the entrance to a wood, with a winding road and figures. *A work of high quality.*

G. MORLAND.

477 A Group of Four Sheep.

A. VANDEVELDE.

478 The Artists Portrait. *Admirably painted.*

CROME, THE ELDER.

479 The Country Road.

WILSON.

480 A Landscape, with ruins and figures in the foreground.

CANALETTO.

481 The Square and Palace of St. Mark's, Venice, with figures.

JOSEPH VERNET.

482 A River Scene, with fishermen hauling their nets; beautiful effect of sunrise. *A capital example of the master.*

JOSEPH VERNET.

483 A River Scene; companion to the preceding.

DE KONINGH.

484 A Bird's-eye View in Holland.

GREUZE.

485 A Bust of a Boy; oval.
*Painted with great force and expression.*

CANALETTO.

486 Scene in the Grand Canal.

WILSON.

487 A Landscape, with two figures bathing.

RAFFAELLE, (AFTER).

488 Saint Catherine. *Copy from the picture in the National Gallery.*

G. B. LUSIERI.

489 A View of Genoa; a drawing.

DENIS.

490 An Italian Scene; a drawing

WRIGHT OF DERBY.

491 A Coast Scene; moonlight.

BREEMBURG.

492 A Landscape, with a grotto, and a Magdalen kneeling at her devotions.

J. AND A. BOTH.

493 An Italian Landscape, with a Muleteer driving cattle to water.

## DRESSING ROOM.

JANET.

494 Mary Queen of Scots, in a black dress and hat.

K. DU JARDIN.

495 A Boy with a Donkey.

EARLY ITALIAN.

496 St. Anthony in the Desert.

QUERFURT.

498 The Farrier; and the Infant Saviour and St. Francis, by A. CANO.

G. ROMANO.

498 Mars, Venus, and Cupids.

ROTHENHAEMER.

499 The Virgin and Child.

PAUL BRILL.

499* A Landscape, with figures.

*End of the Fifth Day's Sale.* Sums £7500.

# SIXTH DAY'S SALE.

On WEDNESDAY, the 3rd day of AUGUST, 1859,

AT ONE O'CLOCK PRECISELY.

## BED ROOMS.

LOT

PARMEGIANO.

500 The Virgin and Child, in a Landscape.

BASSANO.

501 Portrait of a Venetian Nobleman, in a black dress trimmed with fur.

CORREGGIO (SCHOOL).

502 Virgin and Infant Saviour attended by Angels.

TEMPESTA.

503 A Sea-port View, with figures

FLEMISH SCHOOL.

504 The Nativity.

WOHLGEMUTH.

505 The Presentation in the Temple. *Painted on a gold ground.*

WOHLGEMUTH.

506 The Circumcision, companion to the preceding.

MARIESCHI.

507 A Scene on the Grand Canal.

F. MOLA.

508 A Landscape, with Narcissus.

## SOLIMENI.

509 The Holy Family.

## GRIEFF.

510 A Sportsman in a Landscape, with dogs and dead game.

## ALONZO CANO.

511 Beatification of a Priest.

## MIREVELDT.

512 Portrait of William Prince of Orange.

## JUANNES.

513 St. John and the Lamb.

## B. VAN ORLAY.

514 Christ and the Disciples journeying to Emmaus.

## A. VANDERNEER.

515 A Street Scene, Holland, by moonlight, with figures and a laden cart in the foreground.

## TIEPOLO.

516 The Saviour as a Pilgrim.

## ZORG.

517 A Shepherd's Homestead, with figures, vegetables, &c., in the foreground.

## S. ROSA.

518 A Landscape with Tobit and the Angel.

## ZUCCHERO.

519 Portrait of Sir Philip Sydney, in a black dress with a lace frill.

## PIETRO DA CORTONA.

520 The Virgin seated with the Infant Jesus and Saint Catherine.

## LUCA GIORDANO.

521 A Bust of a Nymph, her hair encircled by a fillet of pearls.

# THE PLATFORM GALLERY.

PACCHIORETTI.

522 The Assumption of the Virgin.

LORENZO COSTA.

523 A Vision of the Cross.

E. SERANI.

524 The Virgin appearing to St. Dominic.

GAUDENZIO DI FERRARA.

525 The Annunciation.

BAROCCIO.

526 The Extacy of St. Francis.

ALONZO CANO.

527 St. Anthony of Padua. *Beautifully finished.*

JACOBELLO DEL FIORE.

528 Portraits of two Saints, painted on a gold background and ornamented in releif.

DELLO DELLI.

529 The Decapitation of a Saint.

TINTORETTO.

530 Portrait of a Venetian Nobleman.

CORREGGIO (SCHOOL).

531 The Virgin, Child, and St. John.

DOMENICHINO.

532 Cupid with a wreath; circular.

EARLY ITALIAN.

533 The Virgin and Child attended by Saints.

## ALBERT DURER.

534 St. Jerome in his Study. The Saint is represented bending over his desk intently engaged in writing; the Crucifix on a table before him; he is surrounded by books, and objects of still life. *The whole carefully finished.*

## STARNINA.

535 The Virgin, Infant Saviour, and St. John.

## FRANCIA.

536 Two Saints,—St. Francis, holding the lily in his left hand and a book in his right; and behind him, St. John.

## MARTIN SCHOEN.

537 The Saviour on the Cross, with two Angels near him and the Creator in the clouds; in the foreground, on the left, the Magdalen and St. John are supporting the fainting figure of the Virgin; on the right, the centurian with the soldiers; in the background, a Landscape.

## IPPOLITO SCARSCELLA.

538 Dido on the Funeral Pile. The pile is placed in the centre of the picture, and on either side are ranges of buildings, along which various figures are grouped contemplating the scene; to the right of the picture a distant landscape is seen.

## GUIDO RENI.

539 The Angel appearing to St. Jerome. The Saint is depicted at the entrance of his retreat, holding an open book and reposing on two others, looking towards the Angel, who makes known to him the divine commands.

*The expression is pleasing, the drawing refined, and the execution careful. A noble gallery picture. From the Walsh Porter, and Saltmarshe collections.*

## MASACCIO.

540 St. George. The Saint is represented at full length, holding a banner in his right hand, and the left supporting a shield.

*A beautiful work of this rare master, in fine preservation.*

## JAN DE MABUSE.

541 The Adoration of the Magi.

## VINCENZIO CIVERCHIO. 1500 to 1531.

542 The Virgin with four Saints worshipping the Infant Jesus at the entrance of a cavern. *A fine work of this rare master.*

## GAUDENZIO DI FERRARA.

543 The Virgin, with the Infant Saviour, enthroned, attended by Saint Anthony and Saint Augustine, who is presenting the donor.

## L. CARACCI.

544 The Holy Family.

## J. VAN ORLEY.

545 The Virgin seated near a portico, holding the Infant Saviour in her lap; through an opening a Landscape is seen.

## F. BEGNIO.

546 The Virgin and Child, St. John and the Lamb.

## GAUDENZIO DI FERRARA.

547 The Virgin and Child, with the Infant St. John. In the centre of a building the Virgin is seated with the Infant Jesus, who is holding up his right hand, and contemplates the Infant St. John kneeling at his feet. In the background a landscape, with the Angel and Tobit.

## RAFFAELINO DEL GARBO.

548 The Virgin and Child enthroned.
*A fine work of the master; exhibited at the Manchester Exhibition.*

## EARLY FLEMISH.

549 The Nativity.—Angels worshipping.

## DOMENICO GHIRLANDAJO.

550 The Adoration of the Magi. An extensive Landscape, in the centre of which the Infant Saviour is lying, surrounded by the Virgin and Saints, who are kneeling in the act of worshipping; and above is the Creator with two descending figures of angels.

## PIETRO PERUGINO

551 The Virgin and Child seated on a throne, attended by St. Peter and St. Jerome.

This fine work, which is in the finest state of preservation, was painted for the church of Saint Jerome, at Lucca; it subsequently was possessed by His Royal Highness The Duke of Lucca, at the sale of whose collection it was purchased by Lord Northwick. It has been engraved, and is cited in "Nel Dizzionario Biografico." Exhibited at Manchester, in 1857.

## PESSELLI.

552 The Life of Joseph. The first part is represented in five scenes.

## PESSELLI.

553 The Life of Joseph. The second part in five scenes.

This and the preceding picture are in beautiful preservation, and may be regarded as the finest works of this rare master extant.

## F. VANNI.

554 A Mother and Three Children.

## CONEGLIANO.

555 Saint Catherine.

A fine erect figure, clothed in green, standing on a pedestal and holding a palm branch in her hand: the figure rests upon a broken portion of a wheel—allusive to her martyrdom. Painted in the artist's best style of colouring and drapery. It is inscribed—IOANIS BAPTISTE CONEGLANESIS OPVS. This picture was at the Manchester Exhibition, and was highly praised.

## RAZZI.

556 Holy Family, with Saint Catherine of Sienna.

## GESSI.

557 Virgin and Child, with St. Francis and St. Rosa of Lima, wearing her Crown of Thorns.

## PERUGINO (SCHOOL OF).

558 The Holy Family.

## PELLEGRINO DA MODENA.

559 The Virgin and Child with Joseph.

*Painted with great feeling and sweetness of expression. From Lady Hampden's Collection.*

## FRANCIA.

560 The Virgin, in a crimson dress, with green drapery descending from the forehead, is seated with the Infant Jesus, standing in her lap, holding a bird in his left hand.

*Painted with great transparency and brilliancy of colouring.*

## STIMMER.

561 The Adoration of the Kings.

## JAN VAN HEEMSEN.

562 The Virgin and Child, seated on a throne, with two figures kneeling in adoration. *An elaborately finished work.*

## PALMA GIOVANE.

563 The Holy Family, with Saints in a Landscape.

## DOMENICHINO.

564 Saint Sebastian.

*A fine striking picture, broad and clear in the flesh, with fine expression in the head.*

## GIROLAMO DA TREVISO.

565 The Virgin, seated on a throne, holds the child who is standing before her, surrounded by several saints, one of whom introduces the donor, who is kneeling. A choir of angels is seen above under a canopy.

This fine work was painted to adorn the church of St. Domenico at Bologna, and mentioned by Vasari in his "Lives of the Painters" as his best work.

*From the Solly collection.*

## ANNIBALE CARACCI.

566 St. John in a Landscape, kneeling.

*A work of great power and beauty of expression.*

## FRANCESCO FRANCIA.

567 The Annunciation. The Virgin is standing beneath the portico of a building, and opposite to her is Saint Bernard; above is the Almighty, and the descending figure of an angel.

*This important work has all the intensity of that religious feeling, so much prized in this Painter.*

## PIETRO PERUGINO.

568 The Incredulity of St. Thomas. In the centre the Saviour holding a crucifix, turns towards the unbelieving St. Thomas, who approaches eagerly from the left; on the right is St. Francis, beside whom the patron is kneeling.

*From the Solly collection. Exhibited at Manchester in* 1857.

## G. BELLINI.

569 The Virgin, seated in front, wearing a blue mantle; she supports with both hands the infant Christ, who is seated on a white cushion, playing with an apple, which he holds in his right hand. A rich curtain of crimson forms the background.

## ROTTENHAEMER.

570 Paul and Barnabas at Lystra; a grand composition.

*A capital work of the master.*

## FILIPPO LIPPI.

571 The Holy Family with Angels. The Virgin is seated supporting the Divine Child; St. John kneels before her; on her left are three angels, holding bunches of lilies—circular. A landscape background.

## ANDREA DEL SARTO (SCHOOL).

572 The Holy Family, with Virgin, Child, and St. John.

## PARMEGIANO.

573 The Israelites gathering Manna.

## LORENZO DI CREDI.

574 Holy Family. The Virgin seated under a tree, with the Infant Saviour, who is extending his arms towards the little St. John kneeling at his feet.

A river with distant buildings forms the background.

*An exquisite work of this rare master, painted with great feeling, and particularly delicate in the silvery tones of the drapery.*

## GUIDO RENI.

575 St. John. *A work of exquisite feeling and expression.*

## VEROCCHIO.

576 The Virgin, attired in a green dress, with a crimson boddice, is seated, and offers her bosom to the Infant Saviour, who turns from her towards the spectator.

## L. CARACCI.

577 The Holy Family. St. John embracing the foot of the Infant Saviour.

*Brilliantly coloured and painted with great delicacy and feeling.*

## GIULIO ROMANO.

578 The Birth of Jupiter. The scene is supposed to be an Enchanted Island, wherein the Infant God is represented, cradled in the midst of luxuriant vegetation; his mother Rhea is lifting the veil which covers him, two nymphs are in attendance, and on either side are the Corybantes, playing on musical instruments. In the distance Mount Ida.

*From the Orleans Gallery.*

## LORENZO DI CREDI.

579 Virgin and Child. The Virgin kneeling in adoration before the Infant Jesus, to whom the painter has given a simple and natural expression which cannot be too much admired. The gracefulness of the blue and red drapery, and the correctness of the drawing, are also admirable.

## BRONZINO.

580 Francisco 1st de Medicis, in a red dress. He is leaning on a table, and in his right hand is seen a medallion of Bianca Capella.

## GHIRLANDAJO.

581 The Virgin, attired in a blue dress kneeling, supports the Infant Saviour, who stands on a red cushion and holds a bird in his hand. Through the pillars of the building a distant landscape is seen.

## MICHAEL COXIE.

582 The Annunciation. The Virgin is seen devoutly kneeling before an open book, and the announcing Angel on the left enters, bearing a sceptre. Above the symbol of the Father shines forth in its glory.

## DANIELE DA VOLTERRA.

583 The Deposition from the Cross. *A grand composition.*

## PARMEGIANO.

584 The Holy Family. The Virgin, with a book in one hand, is seated, supporting on her lap the Infant Christ, whom the young St. John is embracing; behind them, the Magdalen, seen in profile, holds a vase in her hand. A half figure of a Saint is seen to the right, and in the distance Roman architecture and a landscape. Engraved by Bonasone.

## FRANCIA.

585 Saint Sebastian at a pillar, transfixed by an arrow; and Saint Augustine.

## SCHIDONE.

586 The Holy Family. The Virgin is represented seated holding the Infant, who is taking the Cross from St. Francis, who kneels before him. Joseph is seen behind the Virgin.

*Admirably coloured.*

## BOTTICELLI.

587 The Virgin and Infant Saviour, with two Angels; on a table, a dish with strawberries is placed, and behind the Virgin, two vases with flowers; circular.

## HUBERT AND JAN VAN EYCK.

588 The Adoration of the Kings. Philip, the good Duke of Burgundy, is represented as the principal of the Magi, who kneels before the Infant Saviour; he is surrounded by his attendants. In the background, the portraits of the Artists are seen through the opening of a window casement.

## PINTURICCHIO.

589 The Virgin and Child. The Virgin is seated, clothed in a crimson dress with a blue mantle, a jewel on the shoulder; in her lap the Infant is seated on a red cushion, playing with the clasp of her mantle.

## SCHOOL OF MABUSE.

590 The Adoration of the Magi.

## BONIFACCIO.

591 An allegorical Composition.

## JAN BELLINI.

592 The Holy Family. The Virgin holding the Child on a parapet; on the right, St. Peter; on the left, St. Sebastian; in the sky are three Cherubims.

*Serious and noble in the characters. Inscribed with the name of the master.*

## JOHN VAN EYCK.

593 Head of the Saviour.

*Painted natural size. A picture of extraordinary brilliancy, and in fine preservation.*

## FRANCIA.

594 The Virgin and Child, with St. Francis and St. Catherine.

*Beautiful in expression, and brilliantly coloured.*

## JAN HEMMELINCK.

595 A Portrait in profile of Maria of Burgundy, Archduchess of Austria, only daughter of Charles the Bold, and wife of Maximilian I. Emperor of Germany.

*A rare and interesting portrait in fine state of preservation.*

## CALLOT.

596 The Marriage of Henry IV. of France with Marie de Medicis.

## L. VAN LEYDEN.

597 Saint Catherine.

## SCHOOL OF RAFFAELLE.

598 A Portrait in profile of a Man in a black cap and dress.

## VANDERGOES.

599 Saint Catherine reading, with the tyrant Maximin beneath her feet.

## P. DA CORTONA.

600 The Holy Family reposing in a landscape.

*End of the Sixth Day's Sale.*

# SEVENTH DAY'S SALE.

On THURSDAY, the 4th day of AUGUST, 1859,

AT ONE O'CLOCK PRECISELY.

## ANTIQUE GEMS, *from the* PONIATOWSKI COLLECTION.

### INTAGLIO RINGS.

LOT

601 Tatius, King of the Sabines—head—*cornelian.*

602 Achilles, in conversation with another Warrior, attacked by Paris with a sword—*sardonyx.*

603 Head of Chilon—*cornelian.*

604 Sabina—a bust—*amethyst.*

605 Head of Pittacus—*cornelian.*

606 Head of Timon, the Misanthrope—*cornelian.*

607 Bust of Anaxarchus upon a Vase—*cornelian.*

608 Martiana—a head—*cornelian.*

609 Bust of Esop—*cornelian.*

610 Bust of Athenodorus—*cornelian.*

611 Ditto of Polycletes—*cornelian,*

612 Head of Xeno of Cyprus—*cornelian.*

613 Head of Aq. Gallus—*cornelian.*

614 Head of Bysas—*cornelian.*

615 Head of Cratippus—*cornelian.*

616 Head of Agesilaus—*cornelian.*

617 Head of Miltiades—*cornelian.*

618 Head of Epaminondas, in a helmet—*cornelian.*

619 Head of Lucippus—*cornelian.*

620 Head of Craterus—*cornelian.*

621 A Female seated—*cornelian.*

622 Julia, daughter of Titus—*cornelian.*

623 Head of Strabo—*cornelian.*

624 Head of Constantine the Great—*cornelian.*

## MINIATURES.

625 F. VANNI............ Ferdinand the II., Duke of Tuscany.

626 F. VANNI............ Guido Baldo, Duke of Urbino.

627 PORBUS.............. His own Portrait.

628 SPANISH ............ Portrait of a Lady.

629 MIGNARD ............ The Duchess of Navarre.

630 TITIAN .............. A Head.

631 GREEK SCHOOL ... Nathan and David; an altar piece. *Presented by the Emperor Paul I. to the King of Poland.*

632 SPANISH ............ A Monk—*in oil.*

633 ........................ Lady Augusta Murray

634 SAMUEL COOPER ... Dr. Bate in a black dress and skull cap—*a fine minature.*

635 ........................ Sir William Temple, in a black dress, with flowing hair.

636 NUDELANGE ......... Portrait of a Lady—*in pencil.*

637 HOLBEIN ............ Sir John Gage, Knight, black dress and cap, with gold chain round his neck; painted on a blue ground, circular. *From Strawberry Hill.*

638 SAMUEL COOPER ... Cowley the Poet, in a brown dress, with flowing hair. *Signed and dated* 1653.

639 PETER OLIVER ...... The Duke of Bohemia in armour, ornamented with gold.

640 ZINCKE............. Sir R. Walpole, in a blue coat, with white wig, enamel.

641 ISAAC OLIVER ...... Sir John Clench, Baron of the Exchequer, in his robes.

642 ........................ Mary Queen of Scots, in a black dress, trimmed with fur.

643 N. HILLIARD ...... Lady Jane Gray, in a black dress richly ornamented with jewels, and a cap on her head, *An exquisite miniature.*

644 ........................ Sir William Hamilton, in a blue coat.

645 JANET .............. Henry the III., King of France—*in oil.*

646 SAMUEL COOPER ... Lady Falconberg.

647 JOHN HOSKINS ...... Algernon Sydney, in a black dress, with slashed sleeves, and flowing hair.

648 SAMUEL COOPER ... John Hampden in armour.

## MARBLES, BRONZES, WORKS OF ART, &c.

649 A finely sculptured Marble Figure of Menandre, the Roman Comic Poet, on wood pedestal.

650 A Group in plaster, of Venus attired by the Graces, on wood pedestal.

651 A very fine ANTIQUE MARBLE BUST of the EMPEROR CHARLES THE FIFTH, on a wood pedestal.

652 A finely sculptured ancient marble Capitol, a fragment.

653 A beautiful Bust, in statuary marble, of Clytia, the daughter of Oceanus and Tethys, on a wood pedestal.

654 *A circular* SLAB *of Italian marble,* beautifully inlaid in mosaic work, with lapis lazuli and other precious stones, 4 ft. wide; on a carved rosewood stand.

655 *A ditto* *ditto,* the top of fine Roman mosaic work, beautifully inlaid, representing Pliny's Doves, with border of roses; on rosewood stand.

656 An Equestrian Figure of St. Louis, of bronze gilt, the head and hands of silver, on a buhl plinth; glass shade and stand.

657 *An elaborate* DRAWING of the SHIELD of ACHILLES, *by J. Henning, jun.*, mounted as a table, on an elaborate stand, and plate glass foot.

658 *A shaped* SLAB *of black marble,* finely inlaid with birds, fruits, and flowers, in Florentine mosaic work of pietre dure; on a gilt stand.

659 *A magnificent Florentine* BRONZE FIGURE of the VENUS de MEDICIS, 5 ft. high

660 A DITTO DITTO of APOLLO—the companion.

661 A pair of square wood pedestals.

## RAFFAELLE WARE.

662 *A magnificent* VASE, with serpentine handles, the belt painted in medallions, representing the Annunciation and St. Michael trampling on the Dragon.

663 *A large lustre* DISH, with a portrait in the centre, and inscription and ornaments in yellow, on a blue ground.

664 *A beautiful* VASE, *oviform,* with griffin handles, and medallions of Cupids and ornaments in yellow, on a deep blue ground.

665 A PILGRIM'S BOTTLE, with mask handles, painted in subjects representing the story of Apollo and Daphne, with or-molu foot and top.

666 *A magnificent* DISH, with the subject of the Martyrdom of St. Lawrence, with the monogram G.O. B.O., (Guido Baldo); on the reverse the description of the subject and the date 1531.

667 A DITTO ditto, subject—The Nativity, with a choir of angels.

668 A DITTO ditto, of fine form, subject—The Judgment of Midas; the sides ornamented with mask heads.

669 A pair of painted wood pedestals

670 A highly finished miniature of Mary Queen of Scots, by Shaw

## INTAGLIO GEMS, *from the* PONIATOWSKI COLLECTION.

671 Head of Calisthenes—*cornelian.*

672 Circe presenting the Cup to three of the companions of Ulysses.

673 Head of Ajax Telamon in a helmet—*cornelian.*

674 Diomed and Ulysses killing Dolan—*cornelian.*

675 Patroclus and Hector disputing the body of Cebriones—*amethyst.*

676 Scipionas—*cornelian.*

677 Lucullus—*cornelian.*

678 Head of T. Testa—*cornelian.*

679 Pythagoras, whole length figure, sitting and resting his hand on a sphere—*amethyst.*

680 Bust of Corbulon—*cornelian.*

681 Head of Pompey—*amethyst.*

682 Domitius—*amethyst.*

683 Pertinax— *amethyst.*

684 Crassus—*cornelian.*

685 Head of Demetrius—*cornelian.*

686 Bust of Scipio Africanus—*cornelian.*

687 Head of Aristeus—*cornelian.*

688 Head of Aratus of Licyone—*cornelian.*

689 Ajax about to kill himself, seated near a ruin—*cornelian.*

690 Bust of Zenodorus—*cornelian.*

691 Head of Pompey—*cornelian.*

692 Ajax throwing stones at the Greek vessels.

693 Head of L. Catullus—*sardonyx.*

694 Head of Aristotle in a cap—*cornelian.*

695 Head of Anaxagoras—*cornelian.*

696 Ditto of Archelaus—*cornelian.*

697 Tiberius—*cornelian.*

698 Drusus—*cornelian.*

699 Pompey—*sardonyx*

700 Head of Sallust—*cornelian.*

701 Flaminius—*cornelian.*

702 Head of M. Plancus—*cornelian.*

## CAMEI *and* INTAGLEI, *from the* GILMORE *and other Collections.*

703 Cameo Bust of Cleopatra—*fine onyx.*

704 Ditto Greek Head, in high relief—*onyx, very fine.*

705 A Comic Mask—*lapis lazuli.*

706 Cameo Head of Medusa—*fine.*

707 The Triumph of Bacchus. He is represented seated in his car drawn by a centaur, with attendants, nymphs, and satyrs.

*This superb Cameo, which is finely composed and drawn, is on onyx of two strata. From the Poniatowski Collection.*

708 A large and fine Cameo Bust of Vitellius—*onyx of two strata. From Mr. Thomas's Collection.*

709 A Bust of Jupiter, in high relief—*fine sardonyx. From the same Collection.*

710 A fine Antique Cameo representing Mercury and Hermaphrodites, with the statue of Minerva in the centre—*onyx of two strata. From the same Collection.*

711 A large and fine Intaglio, representing Sarpedon wounded, carried by two Trojan warriors, encountered by Hector—*cornelian. Prince Poniatowski.*

712 Another. Machaon wounded in the shoulder by Paris—*cornelian. Poniatowski.*

713 Another. Neptune, availing himself of the sleep of Jupiter, appearing to Agamemnon, Ulysses, and Diomed — *chrysolite. Poniatowski.*

714 Another. Lycurgus, King of Thrace, bound to a tree, as a punishment for his opposition to Bacchus, is destroyed by wild horses —*cornelian.*

715 The Triumph of Julius Cæsar—*intaglio, niccolo.* Head of Pompey —*cornelian;* and one other.

716 A large and fine Cameo Head of Napoleon, in high relief—*onyx.*

717 An ancient carved Ivory Scent Bottle, with busts in relief.

718 A large and fine Intaglio, representing Helen, Paris, and Hector —*onyx.*

719 A Bust in Cameo of Ariadne, in high relief—*sardonyx.*

720 A ditto of Mercury—*sardonyx*—set as a locket.

721 A ditto—*cornelian.*

722 A ditto of Apollo—*onyx.*

*End of the Seventh Day's Sale.*

# EIGHTH DAY'S SALE.

On FRIDAY, the 5th day of AUGUST, 1859,

AT ONE O'CLOCK PRECISELY.

## MINIATURES.

LOT

723 SPENCER ........... Mary Anne Brudenell, Countess of Shrewsbury

724 HOSKINS ........... Sir Robert Gayer, of Stoke, Buckingham.

725 SAMUEL COOPER ... Sir Samuel Moreland, in a brown dress, with flowing hair.

726 ........................ An enamel of the Marquis de Vienville, killed at the Battle of Auburn Chase.

*From the Portland and Strawberry Hill Collections.*

727 ZINCKE.............. Matilde, Queen of Denmark—*enamel.*

728 PETITOT ........... Louis Dauphin, son of Louis XIV., set in gold as a locket.

729 ........................ An enamel of a Lady, in a blue dress, time of George I.

730 BÖIT.................. Portrait of a Gentleman in a brown dress—*enamel.*

731 PETITOT ........... Fouquet, in a black dress and cap.

732 SAMUEL COOPER ... Portrait of Mary, sole daughter of General Fairfax.

733 OLIVER.............. Sir Thomas Wentworth, Earl of Strafford.

734 SAMUEL COOPER ... Portrait of the Earl of Sandwich.

735 ZINCKE.............. An enamel Portrait of a Gentleman in a blue dress, set as a locket.

736 ......... ............. A miniature in oil of an Officer of the time of the Commonwealth, supposed to be General Lambert.

737 SAMUEL COOPER ... Portrait of a Youth in a brown dress.

738 GERARD HOET ...... A miniature in oil, representing Venus and Cupid.

739 WALKER ........... General Ireton in armour.

740 ISAAC OLIVER ...... Portrait of the celebrated Dr. Donne in a black dress with frill.

741 J. S. LIOTARD ...... A miniature of a Lady.

742 PHILIP HERBERT ... Earl of Pembroke.

## ANTIQUE GEMS.

743 Thetis in the Council of the Gods seated near Minerva, Jupiter and Juno—*fine amethyst.*

744 Another—Chiron driving the Wild Beast from Peleus—*fine jade.*

745 Another—Hercules presenting to Omphale the Axe of Hippolita, Queen of the Amazons—*amethyst*

746 An intaglio—Head of Horatius—*amethyst.*

747 A cameo Bust of Minerva—*onyx. Poniatowski.*

748 A ditto ditto, Alexander the Great—*onyx.*

749 An intaglio—Neptune in his Chariot—*niccolo.*

750 Minerva and Apollo in the beech tree observing Nestor, who is placing on the helmet of Agememnon the names of the Greek warriors, one of whom was to fight with Hector, *a magnificent cameo on onyx of three strata. Poniatowski.*

751 Aurora in her Car drawn by two horses, *a fine cameo on onyx of two strata, beautifully applied to give effect to the subject. Poniatowski.*

752 Head of Ceres, with the cornucopia and inscription around—*sardonyx. Gilmore.*

753 Head of a Bacchante, set as a locket—*jasper onyx. Gilmore.*

754 Head of Alexander, the reverse Darius, *very fine sardonyx of great perfection. From Lord Crewe's Collection.*

755 Head of Mercury, a fine cameo—*sardonyx of three strata*, mounted as a brooch.

756 Head of Young Bacchus, cameo—*sardonyx*, set as a locket.

757 A Lusus Naturæ of Egyptian pebble, set round with imitative brilliants.

758 A Tragic Mask, a fine antique cameo—*pebble.*

759 A figure of a Priapus, in green jade, the pedestal of silver—*a fine antique work.*

760 A fine intaglio—A Warrior with a Helmet—*sardonyx.*

## BRONZES AND WORKS OF ART.

761 *A superb* SLAB of ORIENTAL ALABASTER, ornamented with designs, in verde di prato, giallo, and other marbles; on a gilt stand.

762 An Etruscan Vase, with double handles.

763 The Mercury of John of Bologna, a small ancient replica in bronze; on a marble base.

764 *A superb* SLAB of ANCIENT ROMAN MOSAIC, ornamented with designs in colours, 5 ft. long and 2 ft. 6 wide; on carved stone base.

765 A gilt Plateau, ornamented with arabesques and miniature views of Northwick Park, and a bisquet figure.

766 A fine Brocadella marble Slab, 32 in. by 19 in., on carved wood stand.

767 *A very fine Florentine bronze group of Hercules and Lychas*, on circular wood stand. 2

768 A pair of Derbyshire Spa Vases, the belts engraved in subjects.

769 A pair of Chinese enamelled Vases, 11 in. high.

770 A pair of ditto, 4 in. high, and a small bronze Barometer.

771 An eight-day Clock, with striking movement, in a bronze and ormolu case.

772 An antique bronze Head of a Roman Emperor, on a marble plinth.

773 A ditto ditto.

774 *A beautifully sculptured marble* CLOCK, with a group on top of Time unveiling Truth.

775 *A pair of fine old Oriental china* JARS, 2 ft. 6 high, richly enamelled in colours, with birds, flowers, &c. in medallions.

776 *A pair of fine Florentine* BRONZES of the GROUPS OF THE MONTE CASALLO; on wood pedestals.

777 A plaster Cast, after Michael Angelo.

778 *A pair of magnificent* ORIENTAL CHINA JARS AND COVERS, 4 *ft.* 6 *high,* enamelled all over in flowers, with medallions pencilled in gold; on gilt stands. *From a Palace at Madrid.*

## MINIATURES, SNUFF BOXES, &c.

779 HILLIARD ............ George Clifford, Earl of Cumberland, in armour, richly decorated with gold, with the motto, "Fulmen aquasque fero."

780 PETITOT ............ Louis XIV. in armour, enamel, set in a tortoise-shell snuff-box, lined with gold.

781 ........................ An engraved Bust of Charles Prince of Wales, and on the reverse the same on horseback, in a shagreen case, with the crown and cypher.

782 ........................ A silver gilt Snuff-box, the top chased in figures.

783 ........................ A small Magnifying Glass in a gold case, set with slabs of bloodstone, and inlaid with mosaic.

784 ........................ A Miniature of a Gentleman, set in a silver gilt locket, chased.

785 BOIT.................. A very fine enamel Portrait of Admiral Churchill, brother of John, Duke of Albermarle. *From Strawberry Hill.*

786 ZINCKE.............. James Brydges, First Duke of Chandos, enamel. *From Strawberry Hill.*

787 J. OLIVER ......... Portrait of Ambrose Dudley, Earl of Warwick.

788 HILLIARD ......... Portrait of Sir Philip Sydney.

789 HOLBEIN ............ Louis the Twelfth, King of France, in a rich dress, ornamented with jewels, painted on a blue ground. *From Strawberry Hill.*

790 MIREVELDT ......... Barneveldt.

791 ........................ Portrait of De Witt.

792 SAMUEL COOPER ... Lucy Percy, Countess of Carlisle.

793 P. OLIVER ......... Portrait of Wycherley, *an exquisite minature.*

794 P. OLIVER ......... Portrait of a Child in a blue dress.

795 SAMUEL COOPER ... Portrait of a Gentleman in a black dress.

796 VANDYCK............ Head of a Young Man.

797 ........................ A miniature of a Lady in a blue dress.

798 ALONZO CANO ...... The Annunciation, a beautifully finished miniature on copper, in a metal frame, ornamented with lapis lazuli, matrix of amethyst, &c.

799 VERTUE ............ King Edward the VI. granting the Charter of Bridewell to the Alderman of London, Sir George Barnes.

800 DAY ............... The Graces, after Raffaelle.

801 LUCAS KRANACH ... Head of Martin Luther.

802 P. OLIVER. ......... A miniature of a Lady.

803 J. HOSKINS ......... John Frescheville, of Stavely, Derbyshire, created Lord Frescheville.

804 P. OLIVER ......... A large and fine miniature of Lady Digby, in an ebony case, mounted with silver. *From Strawberry Hill.*

805 OLIVER ............ Head of a Youth.

806 OLIVER ............ Head of a Sleeping Child.

807 MIREVELDT. ......... A Miniature of Prince Maurice in Armour.

808 SAMUEL COOPER, 1649 ......... Portrait of Richard Cromwell, in an exquisite gold enamelled case.

809 ........................ A Case containing five miniatures.

810 ........................ A frame containing 10 miniatures beautifully finished by Reade, viz.—Queen Mary, Queen Elizabeth, Edward VI., Henry VIII. and his six wives.

811 DENNING ........... Archbishop of Trieste, after Vandyck.

812 DENNING ......... Interior with three boors, after Ostade.

813 DENNING ......... Portrait of Snyders, after Vandyck.

814 DENNING ........... Mars, Venus, and Cupid, after Rubens.

815 ........................ Saint Catherine, after Raffaelle.

816 BOUT & BODEWYNS A small Landscape and Figures.

817 ........................ An Ancient Chasing in a frame, of Edward Howard, Earl of Surrey.

## ANTIQUE GEMS.

818 Liberty, a whole length figure, with attributes.

819 Æneas throwing a Stone at Achilles—*amethyst.*

820 Ceres crowning Bacchus, *a fine cameo—onyx.*

821 Pallas touching Ulysses with her golden wand.

822 Achilles placing his hair in the hand of the body of Patroclus—*cornelian.*

823 Eratosthenes—*cornelian.*

824 Hesiod—*amethyst.*

825 Anachreon—*cornelian.*

826 Therpandre—*cornelian.*

827 Diodorus Siculus—*cornelian.*

828 Plutarchus—*cornelian.*

829 Stesichorus—*cornelian.*

830 Tyrtheus—*sardonyx.*

831 Pausanias—*cornelian.*

*End of the Eighth Day's Sale.* £1664.

# NINTH DAY'S SALE.

On TUESDAY, the 9th day of AUGUST, 1859,

AT ONE O'CLOCK PRECISELY.

## VESTIBULE.

### A. DA FIESOLE.

832 Two Angels.

### GIOTTO.

833 St. Dominic and St. Thomas d'Aquinas—a pair.

### RUBENS.

834 Portrait in profile of Mademoiselle Lundens.

### ALTISSINO.

835 A Portrait in profile of Giovanni de Medicis.

### SIMONE DA PESARO.

836 The Holy Family reposing, in a Landscape. *From the Coesvelat Collection.*

### HOLBEIN.

837 Portrait of Mary Queen of Scots.

### HOLBEIN.

838 Portrait of Henry the Eighth.

### VEROCCHIO.

839 The Virgin, contemplating the Infant Jesus, who is held by an Angel.

### LUCAS KRANACH.

840 Saints at their devotions.

## GIOTTO.

841 The Presentation in the Temple.
*A beautiful specimen of this rare master—small.*

## JAN DE MABUSE.

842 The Wise Men's Offering.
*Rich in colour and elaborate in its details.*

## COSIMO ROSELLI.

843 The Virgin seated with the Infant Saviour and four angels worshipping.

## LUCAS KRANACH.

844 Portrait of the Elector of Saxony.

## ANDREA MANTEGNA.

845 The Virgin with the Infant Jesus, seated on a throne, richly adorned with cloth of gold; St. Christopher and St Sebastian are standing on either side.

## MARINARI.

846 Portrait of Leonora di Toledo.

## KRANACH.

847 The Virgin and Child, with figures worshipping.

## GAUDENZIO DI FERRARA.

848 The Virgin and Child, with St. John, St. George, and St. Margaret.

## ALBERTINELLI.

849 The Annunciation.

## P. DA COSIMO.

850 The Virgin and Child enthroned, attended by Saint Paul, St. John, St. George, and St. Nicholas.

## GIOTTO.

851 The Holy Family with Saints.

## REMBRANDT VAN RHYN.

852 A Pair—Portraits of the Burgomaster Six, and his Wife.
*From the collection of Sir Simon Clarke.*

## DOMENICO PULIGO.

853 The Virgin and Child.

## BAROCCIO.

854 The taking down from the Cross.

## THOMASO STEFANO.

855 The Salutation; a pair.

## GIULIO ROMANO.

856 Mount Parnassus. Apollo and the Muses, accompanied by a number of other figures said to be intended for the immortalized Poets.

## ALTISSIMO.

857 Portrait in profie of Antonius di Lêva, the celebrated Spanish General.

## GIOTTO.

858 The Virgin and Child with Saints.

## PALMA VECCHIO.

859 The Virgin and Child, with Saint George and Saint Lucca.

## INNOCENZIO DA IMOLA.

860 The Marriage of St. Catherine.

## H. VANDER GOES.

861 The Salutation and the Presentation in the Temple, with Saints on the reverse; a pair.

## BENOZZO GOZZOLI.

862 Head of the Saviour surrounded by Cherubim.

## CORREGGIO.

863 Study for the head of a Cherub.

## ROGER OF BRUGES.

864 A Triptique. The centre represents the Adoration of the Magi, who are seen in the foreground of the picture presenting their gifts to the Infant Saviour; to the right, in a courtyard, they are again seen preparing to depart, accompanied by their attendants. The wings represent the Nativity and the Circumcision.

*A beautiful work, in a fine state of preservation.*

## VAN SOMER.

865 The Queen of Bohemia in a richly jewelled dress, with a frill round her neck.

... ... ...

866 An old fresco Portrait of a Woman in a large white ruff.

## HANS SCHAUFLEIN.

867 Portrait of a Reformer.

## GENTILE DI FABRIANO.

868 The Virgin kneeling, in a landscape, with three Angels presenting to her the Infant Jesus. The background is composed of carnations, roses, and lilies.

*A beautiful work of this rare master, and in the finest state of preservation.*

## GIROLAMO DI SANTA CROCE.

869 The Resurrection. The Saviour just risen from the Tomb, on which he stands, holds in his left hand a banner, while the right is raised as in the act of blessing; behind are two Angels praying; and to the left, near the tomb, is Mary Magdalen. A richly diversified landscape forms the background.

*From the Solly Collection.*

## LUCAS VAN LEYDEN.

870 Mary Magdalen amidst the pleasures of the World.

A quaint old painting—the figures in the costume of the time; interesting as illustrating the state of the arts in Holland in the early part of the sixteenth century, and valuable on account of the rarity of the easel pictures of this artist.

*This subject is etched by the master.*

BUFFALMACCO.

871 The Virgin and Child. *A fine example of this rare master.*

BAROCCIO.

872 The Ecstasy of Saint Francis.
*A richly coloured and highly-finished work.*

HANS HOLBEIN.

873 Portraits of a Gentleman and Lady in the costume of the Low Countries.

## THE GIOTTO ROOM.

AMBROGIO LORENZETTI.

874 A Triptique. The Virgin and Child, with two Angels in the centre, and Saints presenting a devotée on each side.

GHIRLANDAJO.

875 The Virgin and Child, St. John and two Angels holding lilies—circular.

FIESOLE.

876 Virgin and Child, with two Saints.

MASACCIO.

877 The Virgin and Child.

HOLBEIN SCHOOL.

878 St. Peter the Martyr.

EARLY ITALIAN.

879 The Virgin and Child, an Angel offering fruit—circular.

GENTILE DA FABRIANO.

880 The Virgin, with the Infant Saviour holding a bird; the background of flowers.

SANDRO BOTTICELLI.

881 The Virgin kneeling in adoration before the sleeping Infant.
*An important work of this rare master.*

## HOLBEIN SCHOOL.

882 Portrait of a Lady in a black dress, with a white scarf over her head.

## GIULIO ROMANO.

883 The Virgin and Child, St. John, and St. Elizabeth.

*A beautiful cabinet example.*

## MANTEGNA.

884 The Crucifixion between the two Thieves.

## SIMONE MEMMI.

885 The Glorification of Saint Ursula with the 11,000 Virgins.

## SAN SEVERINO.

886 The Virgin and Child, with Angels and Saints worshipping.

## DOMENICHINO.

887 The Canonization of Saints.

## LUCAS VAN LEYDEN.

888 The Adoration of the Magi. The Virgin is represented with the Infant Saviour, and attended by Joseph; one of the Magi is kneeling before them presenting a gold cup to the Saviour; behind him are the two other Kings, with a number of attendants and spectators.

*A beautiful work, inimitable in the finish and perfection of its details, and in a fine state of preservation.*

## MEISTER WILHELM, OF COLOGNE.

889 The Vision of Saint Gregory.

The Pope and his attendant priests are kneeling at the altar, where the miracle is exposed to view. On the left side of the picture are St. Gerion, St. Peter the Hermit, the Mother of the Maccabees (with her martyred sons), St. John the Baptist, the Holy Virgin, &c.; and on the other side are St. Joseph, St. Helena, St. Ursula (with three out of her 11,000 Virgins), the sainted Queen of Hungary, and St. Barbara, holding in her hand the tower in which she so barbarously suffered martyrdom. In front of the altar are the Donataire, or patron for whom the picture was painted, with one son, and on the other side, his lady and five daughters.

## TIMOTEO DELLA VITE.

890 The taking down from the Cross. At the foot of the Cross the Virgin, clothed in a blue mantle, descending from the foreground, is seated, holding the dead body of the Saviour on her knees, supported by St. John and the Magdalen. In the background are St. Francis and St. Bernard; a Landscape is seen in the distance.

*A fine example of this rare master, and beautifully preserved.*

... ... ...

890* Portrait of St. Louis IX. King of France. He is represented standing, holding a sceptre, habited in a gold suit of armour; two female saints are kneeling at his feet.

## G. VAN MEIRE.

891 The Presentation in the Temple.

## ADAM ELSHEIMER.

892 St. John preaching to the Multitude—a composition of numerous figures.

## HANS HEMMELINCK.

893 The Marriage of Saint Agnes—Saint Catherine offering Flowers.

## GIOTTO.

894 The Death of the Virgin.

This noble picture is incomparably the finest example of the early Italian school in Thirlestane House—beautiful though many of the examples contained therein undoubtedly are—and from its fine state of preservation and the brilliancy of its colours, must prove an object of peculiar interest to those who wish to study high art in its earliest and purest conditions of development. The subject of the picture represents the outstretched figure of the Virgin, wrapped in a blue mantle, placed upon a couch, or bier, covered with bright scarlet drapery. The countenance placid, though pallid, in death—the eyes closed, and the hands crossed over the body. Around are the eleven Apostles kneeling, with their faces directed heaven-ward, gazing intently and with expressions of profound awe at the figure of the Saviour, which—enclosed in an ellipticle aureole—supported by angels, appears above, holding in His hands a white cloth, or napkin, on which is represented the soul of the Virgin, just received into glory, in the likeness of a little child. On the left hand of the picture stands the figure of St. Lawrence, with his familiar attribute, the gridiron; and at the opposite side, that of St. Stephen, carrying the censer, and recognised by the stones placed on his head and shoulders. The background represents a mountainous landscape, in which are introduced several castellated buildings. The whole subject is treated in a bold and striking manner, full of character, and with a dignity and grandeur every way worthy the reputation of its great master.

MARTIN SCHOEN.

895 Saint Barbara brought before her Pagan Father.

A. DURER.

896 Kings and Sovereigns adoring the name of Jesus.
*From the Bernal Collection.*

FRANCESCO GRANACCI.

897 The Annunciation; under a richly decorated portico the Virgin is standing, and before her an angel kneeling, presenting to her a lily; to the left another angel in the attitude of prayer; above them, the Creator is seen surrounded by Cherubim; a distant landscape with buildings forms the background.
*A beautiful composition.*

BALDOVINETTI.

898 The Virgin and Child.

L. CRANACH.

899 The Archduchess Jeanne la Folle and her Infant Son, afterwards Charles the Fifth.

ZANOTTI.

900 The Holy Family.

GIOTTO.

901 Christ bearing his Cross.

STEFANO.

902 The Virgin adoring the Infant Jesus, and an Angel.

A. DURER.

903 Portrait of a Lady, in a rich costume, holding an apple.

SIMONE MEMMI.

904 The Virgin and Child, with two Saints.

F. PORBUS.

905 The Virgin and Child seated, with a Temple in the background, and in front portraits of Henry the Fourth of France, his Family, and distinguished Personages of his Court.
*A very curious and highly interesting work.*

## HANS HOLBEIN.

906 Henry the Eighth in a rich dress, one hand holding a glove and the other resting on his dagger. *From Stowe.*

## ZUCCHERO.

907 Queen Elizabeth in a rich dress, holding a fan. *From Stowe.*

## JAN DE MABUSE.

908 The Emperor Charlemagne, bust in profile, seen through a richly ornamented casement; he is represented with a crown on his head, wearing a cuirass and a mantle, on which is inscribed "Carolus Magus, Roma Imperatore."

*An extraordinary portrait, considered to be unique.*

## CORREGGIO.

909 The Virgin and Child; the Virgin seated in a landscape with the Infant upon her lap, is looking down with an affectionate smile upon the Infant, and pressing one of its extended arms to her breast, her left hand applied to the left hand of the child, touches the extremities of its fingers, thus balancing it in its seat.

*This beautiful work formerly adorned the collection of the late Lord Radstock.*

## M. VENUSTI.

910 Alpha and Omega,—the First and the Last.

*An admirable work, painted with great force of colouring and design.*

## RAFFAELLE.

911 The Coronation of the Virgin, with the Twelve Apostles round the Tomb.

The tomb below is filled with flowers, and around it the Twelve Apostles, John and his brother James in front looking up; St. Thomas holds the girdle looking up to the throne set in heaven, whereon the Virgin sits beside her divine Son, and with joined hands and eyes meekly cast down, bends to receive the golden coronet he is about to place on her brow; eight seraphim hover above her head; on the left an angel strikes the tambourine; on the right another sounds the viol. The legend relates that when the Madonna ascended into heaven in the sight of the Apostles, Thomas was absent; but after three days he returned, and doubting the truth of her glorious translation, he desired that her tomb should be opened, which was done, and lo! it was found full of flowers springing up; then the Virgin, taking pity on his weakness and want of faith, threw down to him her girdle, that this tangible proof remaining in his hands might remove all doubts for ever from his mind.

*This fine Picture was painted for the Monastery of St. Francisco in Perugia, as recited in the works of Vasari and Duppa.*

## BRONZINO.

912 Portrait of Bianca Capella, Grand Duchess of Tuscany.
*From the Bernal Collection.*

## FRANCESCO FRANCIA.

913 The Virgin and Child, St. Lawrence, and Pope Sixtus.

## WOHLGEMUTH.

914 The Flight into Egypt.

## CAROTTI.

915 The Virgin holding the Infant Saviour, standing on a slab; an open book is near.

## F. VENANZI.

916 Abraham's Dream.

## PIERINO DEL VAGA.

917 The Virgin and Child with St. John and three Angels.
*A beautiful composition by this admired pupil of Raffaelle.*

## RAFFAELLE.

918 The Virgin and Child, St. Elizabeth, St. John, and Joseph in a landscape.

## MEISTER WILHELM, OF COLOGNE.

919 The Presentation in the Temple.
*A beautiful cabinet example of this rare master.*

## PINTURICCHIO.

920 The Adoration of the Kings.

## ALBERT DURER.

921 The Crucifixion between the two Thieves.

## L. DA VINCI.

922 The Virgin with the Infant Saviour seated, in a Landscape.

## BERNARD VAN ORLEY.

923 The Last Supper.—The expression of the countenances is rendered with great truth.

PINTURICCHIO.

924 The Nativity.—A grand Landscape, in the foreground of which Joseph is seated, leaning on his staff; near him the Virgin kneeling, with her hands joined, contemplates the Infant Christ, who is held by an Angel before her; behind them, St. John kneeling on one knee, and three shepherds, who have brought their offerings.

*A noble work of art, which is said to have been formerly borne as a banner through the streets of Florence at the celebration of the religious Festivals of Christmas and Easter.*

GHIRLANDAJO.

925 The Virgin and St. John adoring the Infant Jesus.

## DRESSING ROOM.

W. COLLINS.

926 The Fish Market—a Sketch.

OLD CROME.

927 A Coast Scene, and 2 others various.

BROCKEY.

928 Head of a Female.

OLD CROME.

929 A pair River Scenes.

BARRY.

930 A Bacchante; a Sketch, HILTON; and one other, REYNOLDS.

CANALETTO.

931 Interior of the Doge's Palace at Venice.

BROOKING.

932 The Whale Fishery.

HILTON.

933 A Sketch; Coast Scene, BONNINGTON; and a River Scene, J. WILSON.

PORBUS.

934 Portrait of a Nobleman in a rich dress.

*End of Ninth Day's Sale.*

# TENTH DAY'S SALE.

On WEDNESDAY, the 10th day of AUGUST, 1859,

AT ONE O'CLOCK PRECISELY.

## BED ROOMS.

LOT

REINAGLE.

935 St. John, after Vandyck.

BAROCCIO.

936 A Female Head—a fresco.

R. WILSON.

937 A Scene near Rome, with monks.

JAN STEEN.

938 A Musical Party, the principal figures being portraits of the Artist and his Wife.

BOLOGNESE.

939 A Landscape, with the Repose of the Holy Family.

PIERON, of Antwerp.

940 A Landscape, with a pool of water and a wood in the distance.

SWANEVELDT.

941 A Landscape, with cattle—evening.

VIVIANI.

942 An Italian Sea Port, with figures.

BACKHUYSEN.

943 A Canal Scene, with vessel and figures.

S. BOURDON.

944 The Repose, in a Landscape.

MOLA.

945 St. Jerome at Prayer, in a Landscape.

VANDYCK (SCHOOL).

946 An equestrian Portrait of Charles the First, attended by a Page carrying his helmet.

GIORGIONE (SCHOOL).

947 The Virgin and Child, St. John and St. Francis.

BORGOGNONE.

948 Soldiers examining a Fortress.

S. ROSA.

949 A Rocky Landscape, with figures.

NICCOLO POUSSIN.

950 The Repose in a Landscape.

TITIAN (SCHOOL).

951 The Pascal Lamb.

SCHIDONE.

952 The Virgin and Child, and St. George.

COPLEY FIELDING.

953 A Landscape, with lake scenery.

J. S. RAVEN.

954 A Park Scene, with felled timber and figures.

LINTON.

955 View of Northwick from a distant hill.

LEWIS.

956 The Great Pool at Northwick, and one other view.

### EDMONSTONE.

957 The Market Girl.

### SCHIDONE.

958 Diana and the Gods.

### MANTEGNA.

959 Christ bearing his Cross.

## GIOTTO ROOM—CONTINUED.

### AGNOLO GADDI.

960 The Virgin and Child, St. Catherine, St. Dorothy, St. Thomas Aquinas, and St. Joseph.

### L. DA VINCI.

961 The Virgin and Child, St John, and an Angel.

### MABUSE.

962 The Wife of Martin Luther.

### PULIGO.

963 The Virgin and Child, and Mary Magdalen.

### JUANNES.

964 The taking down from the Cross.

### GENTILE DA FABRIANO.

965 The Nativity.

### L. VAN LEYDEN.

966 The Adoration of Kings and Saints.

### SANDRO BOTTICELLI.

967 The Virgin and the Infant Saviour, with two Angels in the background.

*The colouring brilliant, with great beauty of expression in the faces.*

## DOMENICO GHIRLANDAJO.

968 A Landscape, with the Virgin and St. Joseph adoring the Infant, with Saints on either side; Angels above are announcing the birth to the Shepherds.

## J. VAN MECKENIN.

969 The Crucifixion between the two Thieves.

## CARLO CRIVELLI.

970 The Virgin and Child and St. John.

## GIOTTO.

971 The Angelic Choir—Angels dancing and singing before the Throne.

## BOTTICELLI.

972 The Virgin adoring the Infant Jesus.

## GENTILE DA FABRIANO.

973 The Adoration of the Kings.

*A brilliantly coloured painting, the details finished with great minuteness.*

## BERNARDINO LUINI.

974 The Virgin and Child, St. Catherine, and St. Barbara reading a book.

## MELOZZO DA FORLI.

975 The Virgin and Child, attended by St. John and St. Benedict—a Landscape in the background.

## LUCAS VAN LEYDEN.

976 A Triptic—in the centre, the Crucifixion, with a female figure kneeling in front, in a remarkably rich costume; figures of Saints on the wings.

## TADDEO GADDI.

977 The Virgin and Child.

## GIOTTO.

978 The Virgin and Child with Saints.

### FIESOLE.

979 The Crucifixion.

### GIOTTO.

980 The Holy Family.

### BUFFALMACCO.

981 A Triptic—The Virgin and Child, with St. Francis and other Saints—*Engraved.*

## THE TITIAN ROOM.

### SEBASTIAN DEL PIOMBO.

982 Portrait of Alexander I., Grand Duke of Tuscany.

### TINTORETTO.

983 The Passion of Christ; a Revelation of St. Bridget. *Brilliantly coloured.*

### SALVIATI.

984 Pyramus and Thisbe.

### SALVATOR ROSA.

985 The Soldiers casting Lots for the Garment of Christ.

Two soldiers, the one helmeted, the other in loose attire, are casting the dice; an elderly female is leaning over them, intently looking on, and appears to take great interest in the event. To the right, another soldier martially accoutred, with a helmet on his head and a spear in his hand, is watching the result. In the distance is a large turreted city on the borders of a lake, surrounded by a wild mountainous country.

*Painted with great breadth and force of colouring.*

### RAFFAELLE SCHOOL.

986 The Virgin adoring the Infant Jesus; Joseph in the background—circular.

### VANDYCK.

987 The Apotheosis of Saint Nicholas—*brilliantly coloured.*

## GUERCINO.

988 St. Jerome with the Angel sounding the Last Trumpet.
*From the Orleans Gallery.*

## CORREGGIO.

989 Venus, Cupid, and a Satyr.

## TITIAN.

990 Portrait of Pope Paul III. The aged Pontiff is seated in his chair, and bent by the weight of years. The head and hands are beautifully drawn, and the colouring brilliant.

*This fine work may worthily rank amongst the best of Titian's portraits.*

## NICCOLO POUSSIN.

991 Venus appearing to Æneas. This admirable picture represents the Goddess buoyant in the air attended by three cupids, her arms extended, and her attention directed to her son Æneas, who stands viewing with silent admiration the armour and arms which are attached to a tree before him, and to which the Goddess points. In the centre a river deity and two Naiads are reclining.

*Engraved by Loir. From the collections of the Prince de Carignan, M. Robit, and Sir Simon Clarke.*

## TIBALDI.

992 The Annunciation.

## GANDENZIO DI FERRARA.

993 Christ disputing with the Doctors.

## MURILLO.

994 The Infant Christ holding the Cross.

## SCHIAVONE.

995 Mars and Venus.

## GIORGIONE.

996 Cupid wounded by his own arrow, preferring his complaint to Venus.

*A brilliant specimen of this great master, from the Orleans Gallery, where it is engraved.* 12

## SALVATOR ROSA.

997 A Hermit seated under some ruins, at his devotions.

*Painted with great vigour and brilliancy.*

## FRA BARTOLOMEO.

998 The Virgin and Child, with Joseph and St. John—circular.

*From the collection of John Knight, Esq.*

## PORBUS.

999 Frances Brandon, Duchess of Suffolk.

## P. PERUGINO.

1000 His own Portrait.

## TITIAN.

1001 Tarquin and Lucretia.

*The celebrated picture, formerly in the Whitehall collection of Charles I., afterwards purchased for the King of Spain, and subsequently carried away from that country by Joseph Bonaparte.*

## GENTILE BELLINI.

1002 The Interview between Mahomet the II. and the Patriarch Gennadius at Constantinople. *A highly interesting historical picture.*

## SOLIMENE.

1003 The Ascension of the Virgin.

## GIORGIONE.

1004 Portrait of a Lady, wearing a turban, and holding a dog.

## COELLO.

1005 Portrait of The Duchess of Parma, Daughter of Charles the V.

## ZURBARAN.

1006 A full length figure of St. Lawrence, with one hand raised, the other holding the gridiron—the emblem of his martyrdom.

*A brilliantly coloured picture.*

## TITIAN.

1007 A Landscape, with Diana and her Nymphs interrupted by the approach of Acteon.

## FRANCESCO BESSOLO.

1008 The Virgin and Child in a Landscape, with St Joseph presenting the donor.

## VELASQUEZ.

1009 An Equestrian Portrait of Don Luis de Haro, with an attendant on foot. Don Luis de Haro, Marchese del Carpio, Minister to Philip the IV., at the treaty of the Pyrenees, in 1658.

*This magnificent portrait may be regarded as one of the finest works of the master.*

## ZURBARAN.

1010 St. Bruno in a Landscape, at prayer, the divine light illuminating his face and figure.

## JAN BELLINI.

1011 The Reposo of the Holy Family in a Landscape; in front are two partridges. *A brilliantly coloured picture.*

*From Sir J. Forbes' collection.*

## TITIAN.

1012 Portrait of Henry Howard, Earl of Surrey.

He is represented seated, dressed in the rich costume of the period, with a black cap on his head, surmounted by a white feather; his right arm leans on a table, and in his hand he holds a dagger, while with his left he fondles a little dog.

*This superb Portrait is supposed to have been painted by Titian at Arezzo, during the Earl's visit to Italy.*

## BRONZINO.

1013 Bianca Capella, Grand Duchess of Tuscany.

## MURILLO.

1014 A Peasant Boy with a basket.

*A sketch from nature, painted with great vigour.*

## FILIPPO LAURI.

1015 Galatea, seated on a Car attended by Sea Nymphs and Tritons.

*From Sir Simon Clarke's collection.*

## MURILLO.

1016 The Vision of Saint Augustine of Canterbury.

The Saint is washing the feet of the Saviour, who appears before him in the character of a pilgrim. From his mouth proceed the words—"*Magne pater Augustine tibi commendo ecclesiam meam.*" This fine gallery picture was purchased from Don Julian Williams, by Mr. Standish, for £600, at Seville, in 1825. It was originally painted for the Nuns of the San Leandro Order of St. Austen, and was sold by them during the troubles caused by the army of Soult, in 1810, to Dr. Manuel Real, from whom it passed to Don J. Williams. The picture is mentioned in the Work of Herrera D. Aviles Guia de Seville, 1832. —*From Mr. Dennistoun's collection.*

## VANDER HEYDEN & A. VAN DE VELDE.

1017 A View of the Grounds and Chateau of Ryswick, near the Hague, in which the treaty of peace between England, Germany, France, and Spain, was signed in 1597.

## ALESSANDRO ALLORI.

1018 Portrait of Torquato Tasso, three quarter length.

## TINTORETTO.

1019 The Portrait of Titian; he is represented in three quarter length in a black dress, with a mantle thrown over his shoulders, trimmed with fur. *A highly interesting portrait.*

## GIORGIONE.

1020 The Virgin and Child; the Archangel Raphael presents the young Tobias.

### CARLO DOLCI.

1021 St. Jerome Reading.

*Treated with great freedom and breadth of expression. From the collection of Sir John Brackenbury.*

### S. DEL PIOMBO.

1022 Portrait of a Lady reading.

### HOLBEIN, AFTER.

1023 Lady Jane Seymour.

### S. DEL PIOMBO.

1024 Head of the Virgin.

### J. PALMA.

1025 The Virgin and Child, with St. Peter and St. Paul.

### PARDENONE.

1026 Cupid Disarmed by Venus. *Rich in tone and colouring.*

### TITIAN.

1027 Portrait of a Lady in a rich dress, wearing a Turban.

### A. DEL SARTO (SCHOOL).

1028 The Holy Family.

### L. CARACCI.

1029 Head of a Child.

1030 Two mahogany picture easels, lined with red cloth.

*End of Tenth Day's Sale.*

# ELEVENTH DAY'S SALE.

On THURSDAY, the 11th day of AUGUST, 1859,

AT ONE O'CLOCK PRECISELY.

## THE PARTHENON GALLERY.

LOT

RAFFAELLE SCHOOL.

1031 The Infant Saviour, St. John, and the Lamb.

VAN ORLAY.

1032 The Virgin and Child.

SCHIDONE.

1033 The Virgin and Child.

BISCAINO.

1034 The Nativity.

... ... ...

1036 A Portrait of Shakespeare.

BAROCCIO.

1037 Angels and Cherubim.

OTHO VENIUS.

1038 Portrait of Elzevir.

JANET.

1039 Bust of the Duke de Guise.

ROSSO.

1040 The Feast of the Passover.

ROSSO.

1041 The Israelites gathering Manna.

F. VANNI.

1042 The Holy Family.

JULIO CLOVIO.

1043 The Vision of a Saint.

RAFFAELLE.

1044 The Virgin seated, with the Infant Saviour on her lap.

A DEL SARTO.

1045 The Virgin and Child, St. John, and St. Elizabeth—painted on silver.

LELIO ORSI DA NOVELLARA.

1046 The Flagellation—circular, on slate.

RAFFAELLE DEL GARBO.

1047 Melchisedeck Meeting the Kings.

RUBENS.

1048 Two Heads of Negros—a sketch.

*From Mr. Carpenter's Collection.*

TITIAN SCHOOL.

1049 The Holy Family with Saints.

GAUDENZIO DI FERRARA.

1050 The Virgin kneeling worshipping the Infant Saviour; the little St. John supported by an Angel and Joseph in a Landscape—circular.

RUBENS.

1051 Mercury, Argus and Io, in a landscape. *Richly coloured.*

## CORNELIUS JANSEN.

1052 Portrait of George Sandys, son of the Archbishop of York.

## TERBURG.

1053 Portrait of Doctor Harvey.

## VELASQUEZ.

1054 Portrait of the Artist when a youth. He is represented sketching in a book some object upon which his attention is intently fixed.

## MIGNARD.

1055 The Holy Family.—*Brilliantly coloured.*

## D. TENIERS.

1056 A Landscape with Water Fowl.

## D. TENIERS.

1057 The Companion Picture.

## GASPAR NETSCHER.

1058 A Garden Scene, with a lady seated holding a little child, and a black page bringing a dish of fruit.

## KARL DU JARDIN.

1059 An Italian Landscape with a ruined building, and two peasants seated near a flight of steps; in the foreground, a cow is standing, two others are lying down, and near them two sheep and a goat and a white horse; a lake bounded by a range of hills completes the composition.

*A clear and brilliant example of the master, signed and dated* 1647.

## DAVID TENIERS.

1060 A Village Fête. A number of peasants are assembled feasting and dancing before a cabaret, to the music of a bagpipe which a man is playing standing on a tub; to the right of the picture, in the distance, Teniers' chateau is seen, with the artist, his wife and family, walking in front.

*Painted in the crisp manner and in the silvery tone so peculiar to this master's works. From the Collection of J. Cave, Esq.*

## CANTARINI.

1061 The Virgin with the Infant Jesus, who appears in the act of blessing the little St. John.

## SALVATOR ROSA.

1062 Xenocrates and Lais. *The engraved picture.*

*From the Collection of the Earl of Besborough.*

## VANDYKE.

1063 The Dead Christ, with the Virgin weeping.

*A work of great power.*

## S. DEL PIOMBO.

1064 Portrait of a Lady in a black dress, with a gold chain round her neck.

## DOMENICO BECCAFUME.

1065 A Landscape, with numerous figures. In the centre, a Hall, in which a Court appears to be assembled, probably intended to represent the subject of Esther and Ahasuerus.

## PLAUTILLA.

1066 The Virgin, Child and St John.

## BAROCCIO.

1067 The Baptism of the Infant Saviour. A clever sketch, a study for a larger picture.

## PARMEGIANO.

1068 The Virgin, Joseph and the Infant Saviour; St. John presenting the Cross.

## CARAVAGGIO.

1069 Christ breaking bread with his two Disciples at Emmaus.

*Painted with great vigour and force of colouring.*

## P. P. RUBENS.

1070 Portrait of Helena Forman, the wife of Rubens. She is represented in profile, with a cap on her head, and a loose white drapery over her shoulders.

*Painted with great brilliancy and effect.*

## PARIS BORDONE.

1071 Portrait of a Lady, with long flowing hair.

## JORDAENS.

1072 The Triumph of Silenus.

## F. FRANCIA.

1073 The Virgin seated on a stone parapet, holding the Infant Saviour on her lap; a landscape in the background.

*Painted with fine feeling; the heads full of expression.*

## SEBASTIAN DEL PIOMBO.

1074 An Altar Piece, in three compartments. The centre represents the Saviour about to be placed in the Sepulchre, with the Virgin and Saints weeping.

*From the collection of Allan Gilmore, Esq. Engraved.*

## GASPAR DE CRAYER.

1075 The Saviour conversing with Martha and Mary. A bold composition; the figures the size of life. The accessories are by the pencil of SNYDERS.

## SALVATOR ROSA.

1076 The Soldiers casting Lots for the Garment of Christ.

## AGNESE DOLCI.

1077 An Allegory of Music, represented by two female figures holding musical instruments.

*Exceedingly rich in colour, and highl*

## ANDREA VACCARO.

1078 The Penitent Magdalen.

## BERNADINO LUINI.

1079 The Virgin seated gazing on the Infant Saviour, who is seated on her lap. A landscape is seen in the distance.

*A beautiful work—the heads and hands finished with the greatest care.*

## BONIFACCIO.

1080 The Holy Family. St. John bringing the Lamb to the Infant Christ.

## MARINARI.

1081 Salvator Mundi.

## VANDYKE.

1082 Heads of two Old Men.

*Sketched with the free and vigorous pencil of the master.*

## ROTHENHAEMER.

1083 The Massacre of the Innocents.

*A composition of numerous figures, the whole admirably drawn, and brilliantly coloured.*

## P. P. RUBENS.

1084 The Marriage of the Virgin.—The Priest, with a ring in his hand stands on the left, attended by an assistant holding a book, and a page kneeling, holding a torch; Joseph and Mary stand before him—the latter is in front, with her left hand on that of Joseph; three females are behind them; three angels strewing flowers upon their heads are flying above.

*A noble gallery picture. Engraved by Bolswert and Lauwers.*

## TITIAN.

1085 Philip II. of Spain, the Husband of Queen Mary. He is represented at full length, in a demi suit of armour, resting his left hand on his helmet, and holding in his right hand a baton.

## PULIGO.

1086 The Virgin and Child, with two Angels.

## MORETTO, OF BRECCIA.

1087 The Glorification of the Virgin.

This noble picture was formerly the altar piece at the Church of St. Faustino and Jovito, at Breccia; in the foreground a full-length figure of St, Bernardino, of Sienna, holding in his right hand a golden circlet, enclosing the sacred monogram I.H.S., and in his left an open book, having the three mitres, which he is said to have declined, at his feet; on his right are St. Jerome and St. Joseph, leaning on his budding rod, and on his left, the figures of St. Francis and St Nicholas; above, in the clouds, are the Virgin and Child, attended on the right by St. Catherine, and on the left by St. Clara.

*From the Collection of Dr. Faccioli of Verona.*

## P. VERONESE.

1088 Catherine Cornaro, Queen of Cyprus—a highly finished and elaborately painted full-length portrait; the costume, particularly the head-dress, of a most singular character.

## AGOSTINO CARACCI.

1089 The Holy Family, the Virgin holding the Infant Jesus, who is leaning on the globe in an attitude of thought, near him St. John with the Cross. *A beautiful work.*

## RAFFAELLE MENGS.

1090 The Madonna of Foligno. *A noble gallery picture.*

## SPAGNOLETTO.

1091 St. Jerome and the Infant Christ.

## VELASQUEZ.

1092 Head of John the Baptist in a charger.

## JAN DE MABUSE.

1093 Portraits of Jeanne la Folle, her Daughter wife of Francis I., and her Son, afterwards Charles V. *A highly interesting picture.*

## NICCOLO POUSSIN.

1094 Nymphs, Satyrs, and Fauns.

This subject appears to have reference to the nurture and education of Bacchus, for a beautiful infant resembling that Deity is seen standing behind a Nymph, who sits on an elevation in the centre of the group; the attention of both of them is directed to a Satyr, who is raising a horn to his lips; a second Nymph sits at the feet of the former, with a large vase in her hand, and two Bacchanalian Boys lying in front, one of whom is asleep.

*Engraved by J. Marriette.*

## A CARRACCI.

1095 Bacchus. A figure from the Bacchus and Ariadne by Titian, in the National Gallery. The god is just alighting on the earth.

*Exquisitely painted, and the draperies flowing and graceful.*

## VELASQUEZ.

1096 A Boar Hunt. Said to be the original sketch of the large picture now in the National Gallery.

*From Lord Cowley's Collection*

## TINTORETTO.

1097 Portrait of Andrea del Barbadicus.

## P. P. RUBENS.

1098 The Holy Family. The Virgin is seated near a bower, with the Infant Saviour in her lap, whom St. John is amusing with a bird attached to a string. St. Elizabeth is on the left of the Virgin, with one hand round the Infant St. John. St. Joseph stands behind, leaning against the trunk of a tree.

*The beautiful work is engraved by Bolswert.*

## PARIS BORDONE.

1099 The Judgment of Paris.

## DOMENICHINO.

1100 Susannah and the Elders.

## ZUCCARO.

1101 Portrait of Spencer, the Poet.

## L. VAN LEYDEN.

1102 Portrait of the Emperor Ferdinand.

## MASSACCIO.

1103 Portrait of a Young Man with red hair, in a black dress and a cap.

## ANTONELLO DE MESSINA.

1104 His own Portrait.

## RUBENS (School of)

1105 The Judgment of Paris.

## TITIAN.

1106 Portrait of Bramante, the builder of St. Peter's at Rome.

*A vigorous and expressive portrait.*

## GIULIO ROMANO.

1107 The Ascension of the Virgin.

*The celebrated work from the Farnese Palace, and afterwards in the Orleans Gallery.*

### NICCOLO POUSSIN.

1108 River Gods and young Fauns reposing.

### COREGGIO (SCHOOL).

1109 The Judgment of Midas.

### SCHIAVONE.

1110 Diana and Acteon.

### PARMEGIANO.

1111 The Adoration of the Magi.

*A noble gallery picture.—From the Farnese Palace.*

### GUERCINO.

1112 A Youth with a Pipe, intended probably for David.

### DOMENICHINO.

1113 Perseus and Andromeda.

### G. TERBURG.

1114 A full length Portrait of a Gentleman in black.

### LE NAIN.

1115 Christ breaking Bread with his Disciples.

*Painted with great vigour, the colouring rich and harmonious.*

### RUBENS.

1116 Portraits of Simon de Vos and his Son—half lengths.

### A. DEL SARTO.

1117 The Holy Family, and an Angel with music.

### DE HOOGHE (SCHOOL OF).

1118 An Interior with figures.

### DIETRICY.

1119 The Presentation in the Temple.

*Painted in the manner of Rembrandt.*

## SALVATOR ROSA.

1120 L'Umana Fragilita.

A strange but wonderfully imaginative composition, painted in a masterly spirit, and with an elaboration of detail not unusually met with in emblematical subjects, and the colouring of a full, deep, and mellow tone. This picture formerly adorned the walls of the Ghigi Palace at Rome; and is thus described in Lady Morgan's *Life and Times of Salvator Rosa*, where we are told the picture was purchased from Salvator Rosa by Don Maria Ghigi, brother to Pope Alexander VII.:—"*L'Umana Fragilita* represents a beautiful girl seated on a glass globe; her brow was crowned with flowers, the fairest and the frailest; her arm was filled by a lone infant, which she appeared to caress, while its twin brother, cradled at her feet, was occupied in blowing air-bubbles from a tube; a child somewhat older, was mischievously employed in setting fire to a wreath of flax twined round a spindle; above this group of blooming youth and happy infancy, with wings outspread *(spennachiate)* and threatening aspect, hovered the grim figure of death, dictating the following sentence: —'Çonceptio culpa, nasci pœna, vita labor, necesse mori.' The label affixed to this painted allegory called the picture *L'Umana Fragilita.*

## GUIDO RENI.

1121 The Virgin contemplating the Infant Saviour asleep.

## SALVATOR ROSA.

1122 Portrait of a Warrior, wearing a hat and feathers.

## BASSANO.

1123 His own Portrait.

## CORREGGIO SCHOOL.

1124 The Holy Family.

## VELASQUEZ.

1125 Portrait of Philip the IV. of Spain.

## ROGER DE BRUGES.

1126 Charles Duke of Burgundy; he is represented in a black dress, with the collar and order of the Golden Fleece, and wears a red cap; in his hand he holds an arrow.

*A highly interesting portrait.*

## MASSACCIO.

1127 His own Portrait, in a brown dress, with a red cap.

JUANNES.

1128 St. Mark reading.

JUANNES.

1129 St. John, writing his book, which an angel holds before him.

L. VAN LEYDEN, (School of).

1130 St. Adrian and St. Natalia

*End of Eleventh Day's Sale.*

# TWELFTH DAY'S SALE.

On FRIDAY, the 12th day of AUGUST, 1859.

AT ONE O'CLOCK PRECISELY.

## THE MODERN GALLERY.

### DRAWINGS.

DENIS.

LOT
1131 A View in Italy.

WRIGHT.

1132 A Landscape, with river scenery—evening.

SIR T. LAWRENCE.

1133 Lady Barrington—chalks.

NASH.

1134 Interior of Bramhall Hall, Cheshire.

D. COX.

1135 A Landscape, with rocky scenery, and figures in the foreground.
*An important work.*

NASH.

1136 Milton dictating his Paradise Lost.

# PICTURES.

## F. R. LEE, R.A.

1137 A mountain Scene—a sketch.

## HUSKISSON.

1138 The Rape of Proserpine. *A copy of Etty's celebrated work.*

## OLD CROME.

1139 A Landscape, with broken ground, and figures.

## DE LOUTHERBOURG.

1140 The Castle of Chillon.

## SIR J. REYNOLDS.

1141 Saint Cecclia—a sketch.

## R. REDGRAVE, R.A.

1142 The Sempstress. An illustration of Hood's famous "Song of the Shirt."

> Oh! Men with sisters dear,
> Oh! Men with mothers and wives,
> It is not linen you're wearing out
> But human creatures' lives.—T. Hood.

## E. M. WARD, R.A.

1143 Voltaire and Frederick the Great. *Sketch for the large picture.*

## OLD CROME.

1144 A River Scene with boats.

## OLD CROME.

1145 The Companion Picture.

## SIR A. CALCOTT, P.R.A.

1146 A Coast Scene with figures.

## A. FRASER.

1147 Rembrandt's Studio.

## ANGELICA KAUFFMAN.

1148 Achilles discovered among the Daughters of Lycomedes.

## VAN SCHENDEL.

1149 A Market Scene, selling poultry by candlelight.

*An admirable work, the effect of candlelight rendered with wonderful truth.*

## EDWIN WILLIAMS.

1150 Christ appearing to Simon Peter after his Resurrection.

*Copy from the celebrated work by Annibale Carracci, now in the National Gallery.*

## FRANCOIS ROCHARD.

1151 Saint Catherine of Alexandria.

*Copy from the celebrated work by Raffaelle, now in the National Gallery.*

## WALTER WILLIAMS.

1152 Scene on the Thames, near Mortlake—evening.

## PARKER.

1153 Halt of Smugglers.

## GLOVER.

1154 View of Ulswater—morning.

## GLOVER.

1155 View of Ulswater—evening.

## VON HOLST.

1156 Head of Christ.

## A. LEU.

1157 A Scene in Norway,—approaching Thunder Storm.

## T. CRESWICK, R.A.

1158 The Mountain Stream.

R. REDGRAVE, R.A.

1159 The Flight into Egypt. Mary meditating on the Prophecy of Simeon.

R. LAUDER.

1160 Christ walking on the Sea.

VON HOLST.

1161 The Fortune Teller.

HULME & WILLIS.

1162 River Scenery, with a Drove of Cattle. View in North Wales.

J. DANBY, R.A.

1163 The Wood Nymph chanting her Hymn to the Rising Sun.

D. ROBERTS, R.A.

1164 Interior of Westminter Abbey, with the Shrine of Edward the Confessor.

D. ROBERTS, R.A.

1165 Interior of the Church of St. Jacques, at Dieppe.

A. FRASER.

1166 The Village Sign Painter.

T. S. COOPER, A.R.A.

1167 A Meadow Scene, with a group of Cattle and Sheep.

*An important and beautiful example of the master.*

GAINSBOROUGH.

1168 The Market Cart.

*A replica of the celebrated picture in the National Gallery.*

S. HART, R.A.

1169 The Quarrel Scene between Buckingham and Cardinal Wolsey, 1st Scene of Act 1 of Henry VIII.

## W. MÜLLER.

1170 A View on the Nile.

*The golden haze of an Egyptian sky is exquisitely conveyed.*

## JOHN WILSON.

1171 A Sea Shore—Morning.

## JOHN WILSON.

1172 Scene off Calais,—Evening. The companion picture.

## BONNER.

1173 John Knox administering the Sacrament.

## T. UWINS, R.A.

1174 View of Naples, with Peasants in the foreground.

## H. W. PICKERSGILL, R.A.

1175 The Falconer. Portrait of the Earl of Bective.

## G. LANCE.

1176 A Portrait. The daughter of the artist carrying a tray of fruit.

## W. MÜLLER.

1177 View of Athens. Figures in the foreground, and peasants driving sheep.

*The celebrated picture.*

## DANIEL MACLISE, R.A.

1178 Robin Hood and his Foresters; a scene from 'Ivanhoe.'

Robin Hood and his Foresters entertaining King Richard in merry Sherwood. A large and brilliantly executed Gallery Picture, which for artistic skill in the grouping and careful attention to the arrangement of its general details, has few equals in the circle of modern art. Most of the figures in the foreground are said to be portraits; the artist himself being represented by Little John, whose stalwart form appears with a fat buck thrown over his shoulders.

## HOPPNER.

1179 Infancy—a little girl seated, fondling a dog.

## DE LOUTHERBOURG.

1180 The Avalanche.

*The celebrated work; engraved in the Leicester Gallery.*

## RICHARD WILSON.

1181 The Children of Niobe slain by Apollo.

In a wild and rocky foreground the fated progeny of Niobe are falling beneath the darts of Apollo, who is seen, bow in hand, among the clouds above. A splendid composition, and conspicuous for that clearness of atmosphere and harmonious colouring for which the productions of Wilson are so remarkable.

## RICHARD WILSON.

1182 Cicero's Villa; three figures in the foreground. The building is seen midway in the landscape, rising from an ample space of water, which flows out at the left hand corner of the picture, and is beautifully transparent.

*The celebrated picture engraved by Woollett. From Mrs. Fitz Hugh's Collection.*

## W. MÜLLER.

1183 A Winter Scene, with cottages and figures on the ice.

## HOWARD, R.A.

1184 Sabrina and Nymphs in the Hall of Nereus.

## HURLSTONE.

1185 Constance and Prince Arthur.

"Here I and sorrow sit;
Here is my throne—bid Kings come bow to it."
KING JOHN, Act iii.

## SIR T. LAWRENCE.

1186 Portrait of a Child.

## H. KOEKOEK.

1187 A Marine View with boats.

## HORACE VERNET.

1188 A Bivouac of Troopers.

### T. UWINS, R.A.

1189 Taking the Veil.

### J. DANBY.

1190 A Coast Scene—sunset—view near Port Maddoc, North Wales.

### E. W. COOKE, R.A.

1191 A Sea View—a fresh breeze.

### W. MÜLLER.

1192 The Bay of Naples, with Vesuvius and Pompeii in the distance.

*A capital example.*

### A. GILBERT.

1193 A Highland Loch.

### H. PICKERSGILL.

1194 The Toilette.

### RICHARD WILSON.

1195 The Lake of Nemi, Speculum Dianæ. *The celebrated picture.*

### RICHARD WILSON.

1196 The Campagna di Roma, with the Story of Diana and Acteon.

*This and its companion, the preceding picture, are regarded as two of the finest works of the master.*

### F. GOODALL, R.A.

1197 The Departure of the Norman Conscript.

### C. R. LESLIE, R.A.

1198 Columbus and the Egg.

"Pedro Gonzalez, De Mendoza, the Grand Cardinal of Spain, invited Columbus to a banquet, where he assigned him the most honourable place at table .... A shallow courtier present, impatient of the honours paid to Columbus, and meanly jealous of him as a foreigner, abruptly asked him whether he thought, that in case he had not discovered the Indies, there were not other men who would have been capable of the enterprise. To this Columbus made no immediate reply; but, taking an egg, invited the company to make it stand on one end. Every one attempted it, but in vain: whereupon he struck it upon the table so as to break the end, and left it standing on the broken part; illustrating, in this simple manner, that when he had once shown the way to the New World, nothing was easier than to follow it."—*Irving's Life of Columbus,* book v. chap. 7.

### UNDERHILL.

1199 The Bereaved.

## COBBETT.

1200 A Coast Scene, with French Market Girls.

## FROST, R.A.

1201 Diana and her Nymphs surprised by Acteon. A composition of seventeen beautiful female figures, grouped with great delicacy. The goddess is represented as having just quitted the stream, and seated on a mossy bank is looking with surprise at the appearance of Acteon.

*The subject is treated with poetic feeling, and painted with a finish and accuracy which have rarely been surpassed.*

## GAINSBOROUGH.

1202 Portraits of David Garrick and his Father.

## J. SANT.

1203 King Lear.

## ANGELICA KAUFFMAN.

1204 Cephalus and Procris, with Cupid.

## E. WILLIAMS.

1205 The Doge of Venice.

*A copy of the picture by Bellini in the National Gallery.*

## STOTHARD.

1206 Amphitryon and Alcmene.

## G. E. HERING.

1207 The Monterone Lake and Borromean Islands.

## PATRICK NASMYTH.

1208 View of Windsor Castle.

*The celebrated picture, painted for Lord Northwick.*

## P. F. POOLE, R.A.

1209 The Messengers bringing unto Job the intelligence of his Misfortunes. *An important work.*

## E. M. WARD, R.A.

1209* The Disgrace of Clarendon.

## DANIEL MACLISE, R.A.

1210 The Marriage of the Earl of Pembroke, surnamed Strongbow, with the Princess Eva.

1.7

This noble picture, was exhibited at the Royal Academy Exhibition of 1854, where it attracted universal attention, and was praised alike by critics and the public. The subject is thus narrated in the catalogue of the Academy:—

"The marriage ceremony was solemnised on the battle field, after the siege of the sacked and ruined city of Waterford; and it was in the midst of of its scenes of desolation that the conqueror received the hand of the Princess Eva." "The picture represents the celebration of the marriage, beneath the ruined porch of the church of the period and its round tower—the triumph of the invading Norman knights—the submission of the Irish chieftians, the mourning over the fallen, and the burial of the dead."

Without these brief notices the spectator could scarcely understand a picture in which "grim visaged war" is represented in such immediate contact with the imposing ceremony forming the principal incident in the scene before him. In the centre, the victorious Richard de Clare, with port erect, and clad in the full military costume of the period, is, with his right hand, placing the marriage ring upon the finger of his timorous and downcast bride, while the left still retains its hold upon the sword sheath. The bride herself is richly adorned and apparelled, and seems far too meek and gentle a creature for introduction into the stern and ghastly company by which she is surrounded. Behind the princess stands her father, Dermot Mac Murroch, King of Leinster,—one of the best and most characteristic figures in the picture in a robe of bright blue; his countenance indicating a mingled expression of exultant triumph and indignant menace; and, between the bride and bridegroom the priest—if such he may be called—is in the act of pronouncing the marriage benison. In the foreground below, at the feet of these leading characters, the dead and the dying are lying prostrate, in attitudes finely expressive—their athletic and muscular forms looking still terrible in death. Among them the figures of an aged minstrel, of a female with uplifted arms, whose countenance expresses the violence of her emotions, and the placid rosy cheek of a sleeping child, are introduced with skill, contrasting, forcibly, on the one hand, with the gorgeous proceedings exhibited just above, and, on the other, with the livid and prostrate forms outstretched below. The whole grouping of the principal action is, indeed, most masterly—every incident introduced telling its tale with admirable effect.

On the left, a number of people are burying the dead, and the black habiliments and sorrowful gaze of a party of mourners indicate the interment at the moment of some one above the herd of common men. These and a number of figures representing the military followers of De Clare, pressing forward to witness the scene, complete the left hand tableau. On the right the mailed and mounted followers of the Norman Earl are —each beneath his own distinctive banner—watching the proceedings; while just below, and occupying the base of the picture are seen the vanquished Irish Chiefs, lowering their arms, and in attitudes bespeaking their fallen state. The artist has bestowed evident pains upon the forms and grouping of these native Chieftians, and has been most successful in their treatment; we know not, indeed, which most to admire, their fine muscular development, or the individuality of character and emotion pourtrayed in their different countenances, all of which is rendered more striking by the introduction among them of the maidens in attendance on Eva, bearing bridal ornaments.

## SIR J. REYNOLDS.

1211 Portrait of Major André.

## MÜLLER (AFTER).

1212 An Upright Landscape, with Cottages and Figures.

## GAINSBOROUGH.

1213 A Landscape, with a Ploughman and two Horses.

## CUYP (AFTER).

1214 A Landscape, with Cavaliers.

---

1215 *An expensive* ROSEWOOD CASE for pictures and miniatures, enclosed by folding doors, fitted with drawers, patent locks, &c.

1215* A Mahogany Picture Easel, lined with crimson cloth.

*End of Twelfth Day's Sale.*

# THIRTEENTH DAY'S SALE.

On TUESDAY, the 16th day of AUGUST, 1859.

AT ONE O'CLOCK PRECISELY.

## CAMEI AND INTAGLEI RINGS.

LOT

1216 Two Warriors, *intaglio—cornelian.*

1217 Cacus and the Bull—*sardonyx.*

1218 Head of Perseus—*cornelian.*

1219 Head of Glycere, with inscription—*cornelian.*

1220 Hercules and Hylas—*cornelian.*

1221 Achilles seated before a Cippus—*cornelian.*

1222 Young Hercules strangling the Snake—*niccolo*—an intaglio of great beauty; in a case.

1223 Head of Paulus Emilius—*cornelian.*

1224 Bust of Vespasian, *cameo—onyx.*

1225 Head of Cupid, *intaglio—cornelian.*

1226 Ditto of Seneca, *ditto—ditto.*

1227 Head of Apollo, *ditto—sardonyx.*

1228 A full-length figure of Apollo, *intaglio—jacinth.*

1229 Male and Female Figures, *cameo—onyx.*

1230 A whole-length figure of Juno, *intaglio—amethyst,* and two others.

1231 Cupid with a torch and butterfly, *intaglio—onyx,* and 5 others, various.

1232 Bust of a Greek, *intaglio—sardonyx*, and 2 others.

1233 Head of Brutus, *intaglio—cornelian*, and 2 others.

1234 Twelve antique Rings, various.

1235 Ten ditto ditto, a mourning Ring, and a Sleeve Button.

1236 Seven antique Rings, various.

1237 Eight ditto ditto

1238 Ten gold mourning Rings.

1239 A Babylonian Cylinder, and 49 Camei and Intaglei, various.

1240 A gold enamelled Miniature Case, 2 Brooches, and an ivory Medallion.

## BRONZES, WORKS OF ART, &c.

1241 A fine Slab of Grey Marble, veined with red, 5 ft. 9 long by 3 ft. wide, on a carved stone stand.

1242 A ditto ditto, similar.

1243 A fine old Florentine bronze of Hermaphrodites.

1244 A ditto ditto of Cleopatra.

1245 An Etruscan Ware Vase with handle, ornamented with a wreath of leaves on black ground.

1246 A ditto ditto, with figures.

1247 A ditto ditto, with double handles and figures.

1248 A plaister cast of Venus and Anchises, in black frame.

1249 A Tazza of Black Marble, inlaid with various coloured marbles.

1250 A fine *old Italian Bronze* of the FARNESE HERCULES, 16 in. high.

1251 A *superb* SLAB *of ancient* ROMAN MOSAIC, ornamented with devices and border in coloured marble, on carved stone stand.

1252 An *ancient* SETTEE *of* EBONY, the back and arms elaborately carved, with loose cushion covered in crimson tabaret, 7 ft. long.

1253 A DITTO ditto, to match.

1254 Three painted wood Pedestals.

1255 Two plaister heads of Jupiter and Hercules, colossal size.

1256 A ditto of Minerva, and another of a Horse's Head.

1257 *A magnificent cameo head of* JUPITER SERAPIS *on fine onyx of two strata.*

1258 *A large and fine* CARVING IN WOOD, representing the SCOURGING OF CHRIST.

1259 A fine Bronze—The FIGHTING GLADIATOR, on verde marble plynth.

1260 A suite of three Derbyshire Spa Vases, oviform.

1261 A large TAZZA of STATUARY MARBLE, 24 in. in diameter, on a wood pedestal.

1262 A fine ANTIQUE BRONZE HEAD, on marble base and wood pedestal

1263 A DITTO DITTO, on wood pedesdal.

1264 A FINE OLD ITALIAN BRONZE FIGURE OF APOLLO, 3 ft. high.
*From the collection of the Marquis de la Grange.*

1265 Two bas reliefs in composition, gilt frames.

1266 A FINE BRONZE of the CROUCHING VENUS.

1267 A *fine eight-leaf* SCREEN of *old Japan lacquer,* with silver hinges.

1268 A HANDSOME SECRETAIRE of TULIP WOOD, richly ornamented with or-molu, masks, and mountings; the interior fitted with drawers, enclosed by panelled doors, with the cypher L.P.
*Formerly belonged to King Louis Philippe.*

1269 A LARGE AND FINE CHINESE MARBLE SLAB on stand.

1270 *A handsome* TABLE COVER of AUBUSSON TAPESTRY, beautifully worked in gold, 6 ft. 3 square.

1271 A DITTO DITTO, similar size.

1272 A very fine Italian Chasing, in silver, representing the Concert of the Gods, in black frame.

1273 *A Pair of Old Florentine Bronze* VASES AND COVERS, of beautiful form, finely chased, with mask handles.
*From the Collection of the Marquis de la Grange.*

1274 A pair of Medicean Vases, in black marble.

1275 A spiritedly executed BRONZE FIGURE of the DYING GLADIATOR.

*From the Collection of the Marquis de la Grange.*

1276 A black marble Tazza, on giallo stand.

1277 An Etruscan Ewer, with shaped lip and handle, the belt ornamented with animals and chimera.

1278 A shaped Slab of White Marble, veined, on a wood stand, 3 ft. 8 long.

1279 A ditto ditto, oblong; 3 ft. 6 in. long.

1280 A pair of beautifully modelled Boys, playing the lute and pipe, of old Sèvres Bisquit, on blue and gold plynths.

1281 A pair of black marble Candlesticks, and an Inkstand.

1282 An excellent Skeleton Clock, glass shade and stand.

1283 A fine Vase of the Blue John Spa, 22 inches in height, on a scagliola pedestal.

1284 Another of black marble, inlaid, 19 in. high, on a scagliola pedestal.

1285 *A very fine Antique Bronze Bust of* YOUNG NERO, on a green marble base.

1286 A Grey Derbyshire Marble Tazza.

1287 *A fine Antique Bronze Bust of a* ROMAN POET.

1288 A ditto ditto, of JUPITER, on black marble plynth.

1289 A ditto ditto, of PTOLOMÆUS, on a brass stand.

1290 A Tazza of black marble.

## CAMEI AND INTAGLEI SET IN GOLD AS RINGS.

1291 A full length figure of Venus robing, *intaglio—aquamarine.*

1292 A fine Cameo Bust of Minerva, in high relief—*chrysolite.*

1293 Mars and Cupid, *cameo—onyx of three strata.*

1294 A Male Figure holding an amphora—a fragment of fine antique work—*cameo.*

1295 A Bust of a Female, *cameo—onyx.*

1296 A large and fine antique Cameo—Apollonidon.

1297 Mercury, a beautiful medallion in ivory.

1298 Bust of Michael Angelo—*cameo.*

1299 Head of Hercules, *intaglio—onyx.*

1300 Bust of Hercules with his club—*intaglio.*

1301 Head of Ceres, *a fine cameo in high relief—sardonyx.*

1302 Head of Scipio, *cameo—onyx.*

1303 Head of Mercury, *cameo—onyx of three strata.*

1304 Bust of a Roman, *cameo—onyx.*

1305 A ditto ditto, in high relief—a fragment.

1306 A Bust of Psyche, *cameo—onyx*

1307 Head of Julius Cæsar, *cameo—onyx.*

1308 Head of a Negro, *cameo—onyx.*

1309 Figure of a Faun seated, *intaglio—onyx of three strata.*

1310 Bust of an Emperor, *intaglio—cornelian*—a fragment.

1311 Head of a Poet, *intaglio—sardonyx.*

1312 A whole length figure of Silenus, and another of a Satyr seated, *intaglie—cornelian.*

1313 Five intaglio Rings, various.

1314 Three ditto ditto.

1315 Six ditto ditto, small.

1316 Five ditto ditto.

1317 An Intaglio Head of Lady Hamilton, mounted as a seal, in gold.

1318 A beautiful AUBUSSON TAPESTRY TABLE COVER, 8 ft. 3 square.

1319 *A fine toned Old Italian Violin* and bow, in a mahogany case.

1320 A Guitar, in a case.

*End of Thirteenth Day's Sale.* £ 1062.

# FOURTEENTH DAY'S SALE.

On WEDNESDAY, the 17th day of AUGUST, 1859,

AT ONE O'CLOCK PRECISELY.

## ANTIQUE GEMS, MOUNTED AS RINGS.

*From the Poniatowski and other Collections.*

LOT

1321 Thetis supplicating Jupiter to avenge the wrong done to Achilles by Agamemnon—*cornelian.*

1322 Head of Nestor—*cornelian.*

1323 Head of Menalaus, in a helmet—*cornelian.*

1324 Head of Paris—*cornelian.*

1325 Chiron instructing Achilles in the use of the bow.

1326 Roikus—*cornelian.*

1327 Calemachus. Bust on a Corinthian Capitol—*cornelian.*

1328 Rabirius—*sardonyx.*

1329 Agamidis—*cornelian.*

1330 Three figures sacrificing a Bull, and another asleep—*cornelian.*

1331 Jason, attended by Ætes, ploughing the field of Mars with the bulls—*amethyst.*

1332 Adonis with a Dog—*cornelian.*

1333 Paris, leaning on his staff, contemplating the Apple—*cornelian.*

1334 Uterpe with two flutes—*sardonyx.*

1335 Quintus Curtius—*cornelian.*

1336 Œdipus unknowingly killing his father Laius—*cornelian.*

1337 Œdipus killing the Sphynx.

1338 A Gladiator—*cornelian.*

1339 Head of a Faun, *cameo—sardonyx.*

1340 Suetonius—*cornelian.*

1341 Horatius—*amethyst.*

1342 Tacitus—*cornelian.*

1343 Æsculapius—*amethyst.*

1344 Æsculapius, Hygera, Telesphorus—*cornelian,* and one other.

1345 Hercules and Anteus—*sardonyx.*

1346 The Infant Hercules strangling the Serpents—*cornelian.*

1347 Peace, a Head—*sardonyx.*

1348 Triptolemus, with his plough, receiving from Ceres the ears of corn.

1349 Three Cupids as Sculptors—*cornelian.*

1350 Eurydice bitten by the serpent—*cornelian.*

1351 Atlas on one knee supporting the Globe—*cornelian.*

1352 Three Cupids wrestling—*cornelian.*

1353 Epimetheus opening Pandora's box—*cornelian.*

1354 Merion killing Acamas—*cornelian.*

1355 Head of Diomed, in a helmet, with the Palladium—*amethyst.*

1356 Head of Philoctetes, in a helmet—*cornelian.*

1357 Hector taking leave of Andromache and his Child—*amethyst.*

1358 Diomed with the Palladium—*cornelian.*

1359 Hector and Ajax parted by the herald—*cornelian.*

1360 Head of Hector, in a helmet—*cornelian.*

1361 Head of Telemachus—*cornelian.*

1362 Hermaphrodite, seated on a rock with the caduceus and the cap of Mercury, with a leaf in her left hand—*cornelian.*

1363 Head of Cimon, in a helmet—*sardonyx.*

1364 Terpsichore, with her lyre, leaning against a pedestal, on which is a small statue—*cornelian.*

1365 Ulysses, leaning on his staff, recognized by his dog Argus—*cornelian.*

1366 Head of Pisistratus—*cornelian.*

1367 Ulysses shooting an arrow at Antinous, who is about to drink from a cup—*cornelian.*

1368 Ulysses discovering himself to Penelope—*cornelian.*

1369 The two Heralds taking away Briseis, attended by Patroclus, from Achilles.

1370 Head of Agamemnon, in a helmet.

1371 Venus, with Cupid giving Juno her girdle—*cornelian.*

1372 Ibiches with a Stork.

1373 A Miniature of a Gentleman in the costume of the period of Louis XV.

1374

## ETRUSCAN VASES, ENAMELS, &c.

1375 An Etruscan Ware Vase, oviform, twisted handles, with two Fauns, one of them playing on a tibia; reverse, a Mute.

1376 Another of similar form, with figures of Hercules and the Nemean Lion; reverse, an Armed Warrior between two heralds.

1377 A Derbyshire Vase, of dark marble, and a light coloured ditto.

1378 A beautifully modelled figure of a Leopard, in variegated marble, on a green marble base.

1379 A pair of Dessert Dishes, of Old Dresden China, white and gold.

1380 A set of three finely modelled bronzes of the Venus de Medici, Antinous, and Venus Callipyges, by G. Zoffoli.

1381 A Plaque of Limoges enamel, representing The Crucifixion, by Jean Rémond; in a gilt frame.

1382 A ditto ditto—The Adoration of the Magi, by the same.

1383 Another, The Nativity, after Parmegiano, by Léonard Limousin, 1539—in metal frame.

1384 Another; oblong. The Triumph of Diana, in gilt frame.

1385 A NOBLE SILVER GILT ROSE WATER DISH. In the centre, a chasing representing the Family of Darius before Alexander, and on the border, masks and scrolls.

1386 An Oriental China Vase, of deep blue and rich glaze, with ormolu mountings.

1387 A pair of oviform Vases, of blue du Roi Sèvres, with ormolu mountings.

1388 A pair of ormolu Greyhounds, forming paperweights; China Match-pot, and an Eau de Cologne bottle.

1389 A pair of bronze and marble Pastile Burners, and a pair of marble inlaid Toilet Bottles.

1390 A small circular Wine Cooler, of old Reisner Marqueterie, on four feet, with carved top. *From Strawberry Hill.*

1391 A beautifully designed GLASS CASE, 3 ft. by 1 ft. 10, containing the Address to Lord Northwick, from the Inhabitants of Cheltenham, expressive of their thanks for his Lordship's kindness and liberality in permitting the Galleries of Thirlestane House to be at all times freely opened to the public.

The document forms a rich and massive volume, the cover being of carved ebony upon a deep crimson velvet ground, ornamented with Lord Northwick's arms in the centre, having the inscription tablet beneath, and surrounded by typical devices and symbols of art, all beautifully wrought in oxydised silver in bold relief, and having also busts of Cimabue, Michael Angelo, Raphael, and Cellini, in silver gilt at the four squares, and at each corner a handsomely chased boss—the style of ornamentation throughout being that generally known as the *Cinque Cento.* The back cover has simply a baron's coronet in relief upon the crimson velvet. The Address, which forms the first leaf of the volume, is exquisitely illuminated by Mr. Shaw, the celebrated mediæval scholar. It is mounted on a handsome Spanish mahogany dwarf bookcase, with gilt enrichments, fitted with six drawers, and on the sides are two paintings of The Holy Family, in carved frames.

1392 *A finely modelled* OLD FLORENTINE BRONZE FIGURE OF VENUS, 21 inches in height, on a pedestal of white marble, with green base.

1393 *Another of* A FEMALE SITTING ON A PEDESTAL—*emblematical of the Arts,* on a granite pedestal.

1394 A pair of Green Porphry Vases and Covers oviform; very elegant, 12 inches high.

1395 *A pair of Cinque Cento Bronze* VASES AND COVERS, exquisitely chased in foliage, and mask heads, 12 inches high.

1396 *A very beautiful* SLAB of RARE MARBLE, designed in patterns, and inlaid with various colours, and black borders, 4 ft. by 2 by 2 ft., on carved and gilt stand.

1397 A pair of Bronze Groups of the Chevaux de Marli, on black wood pedestals with or-molu bands.

1398 A pair of square Wood Pedestals.

1399 A handsome Black Marble Inkstand, inlaid with various marbles.

1400 *A pair of very elegant* EWERS of BRONZE, the handles formed by figures of panthers, and the belts chased in subjects after Fiamingo—13 inches high.

1401 A fine Etruscan Amphora, with double handles, a female figure driving a chariot; and on the reverse, warriors.

1402 A ditto ditto, with lions attacking a stag and a bull in frieze on the shoulder, and eyes on each side of the handle.

1403 A Casket of Ebony, ornamented with ormolu, with four columns of the same, and on the top, a slab of fine pietra dura mosaic.

1404 A Bronze Inkstand of cinque cento design, and a black marble card tray with border of flowers.

1405 Three Derbyshire Spa Vases.

1406 A well executed Marble Head of a Child.

1407 *A fine* OLD FLORENTINE BRONZE of the FARNESE HERCULES.
*From the Collection of the Marquis de la Grange.*

1408 A ditto ditto, a Faun carrying a Kid.

1409 *A beautiful* TABLE of BLACK MARBLE, octagon shaped, the top inlaid with musical trophies and border of flowers, on circular stem and tripod feet.

1410 A copy of the Portland Vase, two black marble Toilet Bottles, three Match Pots, and a Stamp moistener.

1411 A small reclining bronze Figure on marble plynth, glass shade and stand.

1412 A pair of Slabs, of Brescia Marble, on carved and gilt stands.

1413 Four Derbyshire Spa Boxes, and a Faience Jug.

1414 A small octagon Table, with centre of fine Florentine mosaic.

1415 A small bronze Group of Cupid on a Tortoise, and another of a Horse.

1416 A large and fine specimen of the Blue John Spa, and a specimen of Petrifaction.

1417 A pair of imitative Porphry Slabs, on gilt stands.

1418 *A fine old Italian Bronze* of the PIPING FAUN, 23 inches high. *From the Collection of the Marquis de la Grange.*

1419 A ditto ditto of APOLLO. *From the same Collection.*

1420 A curious two-handled Etruscan Vase, with figures; on one side Bacchus between two Menades, the three borne on the shoulders of three Fauns; reverse, Hercules, Minerva, and Mercury.

1421 Another, with Hercules leading a Bull, and Minerva standing near an altar; reverse, Bacchus between two Satyrs.

1422 An Amboyna Wood Casket for gems, fitted with sliding trays and drawer under, patent lock, and leather cover for the same.

1423 An ancient Etruscan Gold Ring, Silver Brooch, pair of Marquisite Brooches, two Buckles, and five netted Purses.

1424 Three black Derbyshire Spa Goblets, and a carved Stag's-horn Inkstand.

1425 A Spa Ewer and Basin, four small Taper Candlesticks, and a Barometer.

1426 A Rosso antico Sarcophagus, and three small Tazzi.

1427 A Box containing about 250 Plaster Casts.

1428 An Indian cabinet, fitted for Coins.

1429 Twenty-five cases of Impressions, taken from Dolce's collection of Antique Gems, with descriptive Catalogue.

## HALL.

1430 A pair of plaster Figures of Venus and Apollo, 6 ft. high, on square wood pedestals.

1431 A pair of ditto, Ceres and Diana.

1432 A FINE EQUESTRIAN BRONZE OF HENRY IV., on verde antique pedestal.

1433 A large square Wood Pedestal, ornamented with bas reliefs from the antique.

1434 A pair of red Scagliola Slabs, on wood stands.

1435 A pair of ditto, ditto.

1436 An ancient Guitar, a Tambourine, and a Flageolet.

1437 Two Rosewood Miniature Cases, with drawers under.

1438 Two ditto ditto.

1439 A Mahogany ditto, the centre and sides fitted with plate glass.

*End of the Fourteenth Day's Sale.* £910.

# FIFTEENTH DAY'S SALE.

---

On THURSDAY, the 18th day of AUGUST, 1859,

AT ONE O'CLOCK PRECISELY.

---

## STAIRCASE.

### CANTARINI.

1440 The Messenger of Love.

### GREEK SCHOOL.

1441 The Virgin and Child.

### BELLINI.

1442 Portrait of Macchiavelli.

... ... ...

1443 Portrait of King Henry the Fourth.

### CESARE DA SESTO.

1444 The Virgin and Child, with St. Sebastian and St. Bernard.

### GIOTTO.

1445 Head of Dante.

... ... ...

1446 A pair—Heads of Females. *Found at Herculaneum.*

### TITIAN (AFTER).

1447 Bacchus and Ariadne.

## MURILLO SCHOOL.

1448 The Holy Family.

## ALBANO.

1449 Diana and Nymphs clipping the wings of Cupid.

## RAFFAELLE (AFTER).

1450 The School at Athens.

## ZUCCHERO.

1451 Portrait of Queen Elizabeth.

... ... ...

1452 Portrait of King Richard the Third.

... ... ...

1453 Portrait of King Henry the Seventh.

... ... ...

1454 Portrait of the Queen of Henry the Seventh.

## GIULIO ROMANO.

1455 His own Portrait.

## HOLBEIN (SCHOOL).

1456 Portrait of a Lady.

## L. CORNELIS.

1457 Portrait of a Lady.

## CIMABUE.

1458 Virgin and Child; and figures of two Saints, B. DA FREDI.

## BARTOLO DI FREDI.

1459 Portraits of Luther, Calvin, Melanchthon, and the other Reformers.

... ... ...

1460 Portrait of King Henry the Sixth.

HOLBEIN.

1461 Cromwell, Earl of Essex.

FLORENTINE SCHOOL.

1462 The Virgin and Child, with Saints.

BERGHEM.

1463 Head of a Bull, life size.

COREGGIO (SCHOOL).

1464 The Holy Family.

A. DEL SARTO.

1465 St. Sebastian with the arrow.

*Painted with fine feeling and expression.*

QUINTIN MATSYS.

1466 Christ Mocked.

GIOTTO.

1467 The Crucifixion.

OTTAVIO SEMINI.

1468 The Holy Family.

CAVALINI.

1469 The Virgin and Child, with Angels.

MANTEGNA.

1470 St Jerome at Devotion.

GIOTTO.

1471 The Virgin and Child with Angels, in a rich frame of the period.

BERNADINO DA SIENNA.

1472 The Holy Family.

CIMABUE.

1473 The Virgin and Child with Angels.

VANDYKE (AFTER).

1474 The Crucifixion.

# THE PRINCIPAL GALLERY.

## JAN DE MABUSE.

1475 A Portrait, half length, of the Duchess of Burgundy, in a black dress, slashed with white, and ornamented with jewels.

## WISSING.

1476 Thomas, Earl of Pembroke and Montgomery. He was employed by King William in offices of high trust, and is here represented in the costume of a Lord High Admiral, three quarter length.

## HONTHORST.

1477 A Portrait, in a white slashed dress and lace collar, with flowing hair, supposed to be the Duke of Buckingham (half length).

## ANDREA VEROCCHIO.

1478 The Virgin, with the Infant Saviour, seated in front of a stone parapet, behind them two angels in adoration.

## SCHOOL OF FRANCIA.

1479 St. John baptising the Saviour in the River Jordan, St. Jerome and St. Augustine presenting the donors, who are kneeling.

## FRANCESCO VANNI.

1480 The Virgin and Child, with St. Dominic and St. Catherine of Sienna. St. Dominic is here represented as receiving from the Virgin a chaplet of beads, and St. Catherine of Sienna a new heart from the Infant Jesus.

## MASSACCIO.

1481 A scene from the Life of St. Francis de Paul.

## MASSACCIO.

1482 The companion picture to the preceding.

## GUIDO.

1483 Portrait of Cardinal Borromeo.

## TITIAN.

1484 The Doge Vendramini. He is represented in his ducal robes and cap. *A fine portrait.*

## CARLO CIGNANI.

1485 Adam accepting, and Eve plucking the Forbidden Fruit.

This fine production is considered by some of the most comptent judges as its master's *chef d'œuvre;* and Malvasio, in noticing it in his *Felsino Pittrice, Vol. III.*, mentions that the Cardinal San Cæsareo, when passing through Forti, where Cignani then resided, desired to have one of his paintings for his private gratification, was shown this Adam and Eve in the garden, and being pleased beyond measure with the picture, gave him for it five hundred pistoles, politely telling the artist that he only paid him for the canvass, accepting the painting as a gift.

## L. DA VINCI.

1486 The Penitent Magdalen. At the top of the picture is the inscription—Melius est sperare in Jehova, quam confidere in Principibus.

## CARAVAGGIO.

1487 David with the Head of Goliath.

## ELIZABETTA SERANI.

1488 The Magdalen in a Grotto, with Angels appearing to her.

## VANDYKE.

1489 Portraits of an elderly Lady, her Daughter, and Child.

## TITIAN.

1490 Portrait of the Wife of the Doge Vendramini—companion to lot 1484.

## GIORGIONE.

1491 A Warrior after a Combat, attended by a page.

## PARIS BORDONE.

1492 The Concealment and Discovery of Moses.

## UBERTINO.

1493 Alms Giving—Scenes in the Interior of a Chapel—and the Death of St. Francis—a pair.

## VANDYCK.

1494 Judge Morton in his judicial robe—*a very fine portrait, half length.*

## SIR ANTHONY MORE.

1495 Portrait of Sir Philip Sydney. He is represented at three quarter length, in a black dress with a ruff and lace ruffles, resting his right hand on his hip, and his left on a table.

## BENVENUTO GAROFALO.

1496 The Annunciation to the Virgin Mary, who is kneeling before a lectern; the Angel Gabriel stands in front; above is seen the figure of the Creator.

*From the collection of Count Orsini of Florence.*

## J. PALMA.

1497 Holy Family, with Saints in the foreground of a landscape. The figures introduced with the Virgin and Child in this picture are St. Joseph, Mary Magdalen, St. Catherine, and St. Jerome—the latter in the act of presenting St. John. A fine composition, with a landscape in the background.

## ALBERT CUYP.

1498 Count D'Egmont. A fine whole length portrait, in a black dress, with a hat and feathers, accompanied by a favourite dog.

## VELASQUEZ.

1499 Don Juan of Austria, son of Philip IV. He is represented at full length in armour, wearing a hat with a red plume; the right hand is extended, pointing to the lines of the enemy, against whom the army under the orders of Don Juan, are seen in the middle distance, carrying on offensive operations; the left rests upon the hip near the hilt of the sword.

## ANDREA SIRANI.

1500 The Conception.

*A grand composition, brilliantly coloured, and painted with great sweetness of expression.*

## RAFFAELLE.

1501 The Holy Family. The Virgin seated in a landscape, holds the Saviour to St. John, who is offering worship. The head of the Virgin eminently beautiful.

## J. PALMA.

1502 Christ at the Pool of Bethesda.

*A fine composition, and brilliantly coloured.*

## MIGNARD.

1503 Portrait of Cardinal de Fleury, Minister to Louis XIV.—half length.

## PARMEGIANO.

1504 Portrait of Balthasar Castiglione. A green curtain draped, forms the background—*a magnificent portrait. Engraved.*

## L. DA VINCI.

1505 St. John with his right arm uplifted, pointing to the cross which he holds in his left hand.

## TITIAN.

1506 Mary Magdalene in the Desert. The character of the head, the drawing of the hands, the cast of the draperies, and the general colouring of the whole are excellent. It was formerly considered among the most precious of Titian's paintings in the Orleans Gallery.

## REMBRANDT.

1507 Tobias and the Angel. The subject is here introduced in a wooded landscape, and the youth is seen sitting beneath a tree with his hat and a pitcher by his side, and the Angel standing near, apparently speaking to him.

*Smith's Catalogue, page* 18, *No.* 47.

## RUBENS.

1508 David with the Elders of Israel, offering sacrifice on the removal of the ark from the house of Obededom.

*A vigorous sketch.*

## PHILIP WOUVERMANS.

1509 The Miseries of War—A Landscape, presenting a view of the seat of war, the whole country being occupied by soldiers; the principal group consists of five horsemen, before whom a boy and two women, are on their knees imploring mercy; various other groups are dispersed over the scene; and in the distance, a town on fire.

*An important work of the master. From the collection of Van Lankeren of Antwerp.*

## ANDREA SACCHI.

1510 The Ascension of the Virgin, with Saints John, Paul the Hermit, Jerome and Peter, standing below.

*A magnificent work, the figures the size of life.*

## JACOPO PALMA.

1511 The Holy Family—St. John pointing to the Lamb.

## FILIPPO LIPPI.

1512 A Landscape, with the Virgin kneeling in adoration before the Infant Christ; Joseph and the Infant St. John in the backgroud.

## GUERCINO.

1513 Jacob blessing Manasseh and Ephraim, the two sons of Joseph.

*A fine work. From the collection of T. S. Cave, Esq.*

## JAN DE MABUSE.

1514 The Holy Family—Joseph presenting fruit to the Infant Saviour.

## BASSANO.

1515 St. Jerome at his Devotions.

## COREGGIO.

1516 The Nativity, Scene in the Stable, with Angels.

## FRANCIA.

1517 The Virgin and Child.

## CORREGGIO (SCHOOL).

1518 The Holy Family, Angels Ministering.

## ECKHOUT.

1519 The Adoration of the Magi.

## LUDOVICO CARACCI.

1520 Christ's Charge to Peter—Our Divine Saviour in the midst of three of his disciples, is emphatically pointing with his fore finger to a cup, out of which arises The Holy Eucharist, which an Angel is holding forward in her hand, St. Peter kneels before the Saviour.

*A fine gallery picture, which may rank among the best of Carracci's works.*

## NICCOLO POUSSIN.

1521 Apollo and Daphne. In this composition Apollo is represented seated on a bank, embracing affectionatly the half transformed nymph; a river deity is seated at the foot of the forming tree, a cupid stands near him, and a second is flying above.

*Formerly in the collection of Lord Radstock. Smith's Catalogue, page* 100, *No.* 188.

## TITIAN (AFTER).

1522 Holy Family with Saints.

## LUINI.

1523 A Magdalen.

## SCHOOL OF DA VINCI.

1524 The Holy Family.

## RAFFAELLE (AFTER).

1525 The Virgin and Child.

## JAN DE MABUSE.

1526 The Virgin with the Infant Saviour.

## ITALIAN SCHOOL.

1527 The Virgin and Child, and St. John.

## RAFFAELLE (SCHOOL).

1528 The Virgin and Child.

## GAROFALO.

1529 Concert of Angels.

## DOMENICO FETI.

1530 The Ascension of the Virgin.

... ... ...

1531 A Magdalen.

## A. DEL SARTO.

1532 The Holy Family.

## CARLO DOLCI (AFTER).

1533 La Poesia.

## L. DA VINCI (AFTER).

1534 Vanity and Modesty.

## TADDEO GADDI.

1535 Virgin and Child, with Saints.

... ... ...

1536 Portraits of Maximilian and the Archduke Phillip.
*A curious early picture. From Strawberry Hill.*

## L. VAN LEYDEN.

1537 Virgin and Child, with Saints.

## DEL PIOMBO.

1538 The taking down from the Cross.

## GENTILE BELLINI.

1539 Mahomet the Second in a red dress, wearing a turban, his right hand resting on the hilt of his dagger. *A rare and highly interesting portrait. Painted at Constantinople,* A.D. 1458, *by Bellini, who was sent from Venice for that purpose.*

## UNKNOWN.

1540 Portrait of the Emperor Maximilian, holding a flower in his hand.

*End of the Fifteenth Day's Sale.*

# SIXTEENTH DAY'S SALE.

On FRIDAY, the 19th day of AUGUST, 1859,

AT ONE O'CLOCK PRECISELY.

## BED ROOMS.

DOMENICHINO (AFTER).

LOT

1541 A Landscape with a bridge.

S. ROSA SCHOOL.

1542 A Landscape with figures. /.

G. ROMANO.

1543 Ulysses and Nausicaa.

S. BOURDON.

1544 A subject from Roman History.

PADUANINO.

1545 Cupid with an arrow.

G. ROMANO.

1546 A Landscape with the subject of Quintus Curtius leaping into the gulf.

GEORGIONE.

1547 Head of a Man.

PASSIGNANO.

1548 The Miracle of Saint Francis.

GAINSBOROUGH.

1549 Portrait of William Pitt, half length.

F. MOLA.

1550 The Three Marys at the Tomb.

VANDYCK.

1551 Cain and Abel. *A vigorous sketch.*

JUANNES.

1552 The Reposo in a landscape—*circular.*

GAROFALO.

1553 The Adoration of the Kings.

ALBERT DURER.

1554 The Infant St. John.

LE DUC.

1555 The Spanish Drummer.

JAN MIEL.

1556 Figures regaling outside a Cabaret.

K. DU JARDIN.

1557 A Landscape with cattle.

... ... ...

1558 Charles, Duke of Burgundy.

BIRD.

1559 A Scene from one of Shakspeare's Plays.

ITALIAN.

1560 The Virgin and Child.

F. WILKIN.

1561 The Reposo. *A beautiful drawing after Titian.*

G. POUSSIN.

1562 A Landscape and figures.

## PRINCIPAL GALLERY—CONTINUED.

### MIGNARD.

1563 The Holy Family (after Raffaelle).

### INNOCENZA DA IMMOLA.

1564 The Marriage of St. Catherine.

### ANDREA SALAINO.

1565 The Virgin with the Infant seated on her lap.

### SCHOOL OF GIORGIONE.

1566 The Riposo in a Landscape.

### MARCO BASIATI.

1567 The Holy Family.

### LUINI SCHOOL.

1568 The Magdalen with the vase of precious ointment.

### MORALES.

1569 Christ crowned with Thorns.

### CONEGLIANO.

1570 The Virgin and Child and an Angel.

### FRA BARTOLOMEO.

1571 The Virgin and Child with the Infant St. John.

### GAROFALO.

1572 The Holy Family—Mary and Joseph are kneeling before the Infant Jesus, placed in a cradle between them.

### A. CARACCI.

1573 The Dead Christ, with the two Mary's and St. Francis.

### P. P. RUBENS.

1574 A Lion and Lioness—*a large gallery picture.*

## ANDREA MANTEGNA.

1575 A Triumphal Procession. A composition of numerous figures.
*Brilliantly coloured.*

## FRA BARTOLOMEO.

1576 The Virgin and Child, with the Infant St. John holding a cup.
*A beautiful work of the master; the expression of the heads admirable. From the Coesveldt Gallery.*

## GIORGIONE.

1577 The Woman taken in Adultery.

The precise moment seized by the painter appears to be that described by the Evangelist, when the Saviour "lifted up himself, and said unto them, he that is without sin among you, let him first cast a stone at her."

## P. P. RUBENS.

1578 The Four Fathers of the Church—Saints Gregory, Ambrose, Augustine and Jerome. These venerable persons are seated, and three of them are attending to Jerome, who appears to be expounding the Scriptures. Three Angels bearing a crozier, a burning heart, and a bee-hive, hover about their heads.

## TITIAN.

1579 The Virgin, Infant Saviour, and St. John, with Mary presenting a Chalice. *A beautiful work, painted in a full golden tone.*

## GASPAR DE CRAYER.

1580 Dance of Sylvan Nymphs. *The grouping of the figures, and the harmonious colouring of this picture are excellent. This was formerly in the Le Brun Gallery, and has been engraved.*

## GUERCINO.

1581 Saint John; his right hand upon his breast, and the reed Cross in his left. *From the collection of Sir Simon Clarke.*

## L. DA VINCI.

1582 The Virgin supporting the Infant Jesus, who is seated before her on a rock, drawing her attention to a bunch of cherries which lies before him; the branches of a jessamine with its flowers form the background.
*A lovely composition; the face of the Virgin full of expression.*

## LUCAS VAN LEYDEN.

1583 The Emperor Maximilian I., half length. He is represented in a crimson robe, trimmed with fur, and a black hat, on which is a golden medallion of the Virgin and Child; in his hand he holds a pomegranite; on the background is an inscription in which the year of his Death is given, and also the Imperial Arms.

## ROGER DE BRUGES.

1584 Louis XI. King of France. He is depicted kneeling at a lectern, with joined hands, and wears a robe trimmed with fur, and a black cap; above him, through a window on the right, is seen a castle, and through a similar opening on the left, a church.

*A rare and highly interesting portrait.*

## INNOCENZA DA IMMOLA.

1585 A Grand Altar Piece, with full length figures of Saint Bartholomew, St. Blaise, and St. Nicholas.

## ANDREA DEL SARTO.

1586 Portrait of a Gentlemen, in a black dress and cap.

## RAFFAELLE.

1587 Portrait of the Duke d'Urbino, in a crimson dress, trimmed with fur, and a black hat.

*A magnificent portrait.*

## ANDREA DEL SARTO.

1588 The Virgin and Child with St. John seated, and Joseph in the background.

## GASPAR NETSCHER.

1589 An Interior—a figure kneeling in the act of presenting a letter addressed á la Regne Regente, to a lady in the dress of an Abbess, surrounded by courtiers. The figures are evidently portraits.

## ALBERT CUYP.

1590 A Landscape, with full length Portraits of Pierre Both, the first Governor of Batavia, and his Wife, attended by a Negro bearing a parasol; the opposite side of the picture gives a View of the Dutch Fleet at anchor off the city of Batavia; beyond which, the distant hilly country of Java is seen.

*A highly interesting work of this great master.*

## RAFFAELLE.

1591 Portrait of Bartolomeo Bianchini, in a black dress and cap, in his hand an open letter.

*A very rare and beautiful portrait.*

## ANDREA DEL SARTO.

1592 Portrait of a Lady, in a black dress, with a veil falling over the head and neck.

## VAN OS.

1593 A group of Flowers in a Vase, with birds' nest and young birds.

*A capital production of the master.*

## VAN OS.

1594 A Group of Fruits and Flowers, with birds' nest and eggs, and a mouse. *The companion picture to the preceding, equally fine.*

## RUBENS.

1595 Portraits of the Emperor Charles I., allegorically treated—he is represented in armour, holding a sceptre, and leaning on a globe, which a cupid holds before him.

## CONEGLIANO.

1596 The Virgin and Child with St. John and Joseph.

## ALBERT CUYP.

1597 The Meeting of David and Abigail. In a mountainous landscape, illumined by the rays of the sun, David is represented surrounded by his warriors, and to the right of the picture, Abigail with her attendant maidens.

## GERARD DOW.

1598 Portrait of the Celebrated Dr. Harvey.

*A highly interesting portrait, executed with all the delicacy and finish of a miniature.*

## GUIDO.

1599 The Penitent Magdalen. *From the Caprara Palace at Bologna.*

## ALONZO CANO.

1600 The Vision of St. Anthony of Padua.

## RAFFAELLE (SCHOOL).

1601 La Madonna del Impannata.

*From the collection of the Rev. J. Sandford, who brought it from Florence in the year* 1838.

## CARLO MARATTI.

1602 Portrait of Pope Clement XI. *From the Lucca Gallery.*

## TITIAN.

1603 The Holy Family. Mary Magdalen, bending before the Virgin.

## VELASQUEZ.

1604 Portrait of Pope Innocent X.

## FRANK HALS.

1605 His Own Portrait.

## LAVINIA.

1606 A Lady, in a brown dress; believed to be a portrait of herself.

## MIGNARD.

1607 Portrait of Peter the Great, in a scarlet mantle, lined with ermine

## ZURBARAN.

1608 A Monk, in Meditation, holding a skull.

## MURILLO, (School of).

1609 The Virgin and St. Joseph kneeling, with the Infant seated on a cradle between them.

... ... ...

1610 Francis de Valois, Dauphin of France, Son of Francis I.

... ... ...

1611 Portrait of Cardinal Granville.

JANET (AFTER).

1612 The Three Brothers Coligny.

## BEAUTIFUL ENAMELS BY H. BONE.

1613 The Holy Family, after Raffaelle.

1614 Thomas Howard, Third Duke of Norfolk, after Holbein.

1615 The Earls of Bedford and Bristol, after Vandyck.

1616 Lady Jane Grey, after Holbein.

1617 Algernon Percy, Earl of Northumberland, after Vandyck.

1618 Sir Charles Lucas, after Vandyck.

1619 The Marquis of Newcastle, after Vandyck.

1620 Lady Hamilton, as Ariadne, after the beautiful picture by Madame Le Brun. *This exquisite enamel was painted expressly for Sir W. Hamilton, and bequeathed by him to Lord Nelson. It is mentioned in Nelson's Memoirs.*

1621 Portrait of A. Hope, Esq.

# BED ROOMS.

## PICTURES.

P. DA CORTONA.

1622 The Meeting of Mary and Elizabeth.

RONTBOUTS.

1623 A Landscape, with a market cart.

BREUGHEL.

1624 Village Festival.

GIORGIONE (SCHOOL).

1625 The Virgin and Child and St. Barbara.

ORCAGNA.

1626 Heralds proclaiming an Edict. *A very curious picture.*

FERRARA (SCHOOL).

1627 Christ in the Garden, the Disciples asleep.

... ... ...

1628 Holy Family with Angels—circular.

BOTTICELLI (STYLE OF).

1629 The Adoration of the Infant Jesus.

CANALETTO (AFTER).

1630 Canal Scene, Venice.

PULIGO.

1631 The Holy Family.

C. DA SESTO.

1632 The Virgin and Child.

MURILLO (SCHOOL.)

1633 The Annunciation.

SCHOOL OF A DEL SARTO.

1634 The Virgin and Child with Angels.

COELLO.

1635 Philip the Second of Spain.

RAFFAELLE (SCHOOL).

1636 The Virgin and Child.

TINTORETTO.

1637 Pope Paul the Fifth.

### TITIAN (AFTER).

1638 Portrait of Titian's Daughter.

### BENOZZO GOZZOLI.

1639 The Birth of the Saviour, and two pictures, after Fiesole.

### CRESPI.

1640 Nymph and Satyr, and a Landscape, LOCATELLI.

### C. DOLCI.

1641 (St. John, a drawing, a plaster bas relief,) and the Virgin and Child.
withdrawn

### ROBERTS (AFTER).

1642 The Destruction of Jerulasem. *A lithograph.*

1643

*End of the Sixteenth Day's Sale.*

# SEVENTEENTH DAY'S SALE.

On TUESDAY, the 23rd day of AUGUST, 1859,

AT ONE O'CLOCK PRECISELY.

## UPPER BED ROOMS.

RUBENS (SCHOOL).

1644 Head of Peter the Hermit.

RAFFAELLE (SCHOOL).

1645 La Vierge au Voile.

BISCAINO.

1646 The Virgin and Child and St. John.

EARLY ITALIAN.

1647 The Adoration of the Infant Jesus.

VELASQUEZ (SCHOOL).

1648 A full length portrait of Philip IV. of Spain.

A DEL SARTO.

1649 The Virgin, Infant Jesus and St. John.

CARACCI (SCHOOL).

1650 The Holy Family.

GUIDO (SCHOOL).

1651 The Virgin and Child.

... ... ...

1652 The Virgin and Child.

MURILLO.

1653 The Baptism of the Saviour in the River Jordan.

PARMEGIANO (STYLE OF).

1654 The Holy Family.

MARIESCHI.

1655 Canal Scene, Venice.

CLAUDE (AFTER).

1656 The Embarcation of St. Ursula.

ITALIAN.

1657 The Virgin, Child and St. John.

DEL PIOMBO (AFTER).

1658 The Virgin and Child.

F. MOLA.

1659 The Magdalen in the Desert.

MARIESCHI.

1660 The Church of San Georgio, Venice.

ANDREA SACCHI.

1661 Pope Clement IX.

ITALIAN.

1662 The Holy Family.

MODERN.

1663 A Coast Scene, with a lady buying fish.

PINTURECCHEO.

1664 The Holy Family.

F. MOLA.

1665 A Landscape, with the story of Narcissus.

... ... ...

1666 The Marriage of St. Catherine.

### CREDI.

1667 The Adoration.

### PARMEGIANO (STYLE OF).

1668 The Holy Family.

... ... ...

1669 Portrait of Edward VI.

### CANTARINI.

1670 The Magdalen at Devotion.

### GIORGIONE.

1671 St. Anthony preaching to the Fishes.

## PRINCIPAL GALLERY—CONTINUED.

### CARLO MARATTI.

1672 The Holy Virgin with a Book.

### LUINI.

1673 The Virgin and Child, and St. John with the Lamb.

### MORALES EL DIVINO.

1674 Ecce Homo. *An exquisite work of this rare master.*

### THE CHEVALIER BAYARD.

1675 A Bust in Profile. *A rare portrait.*

### GONZALES COQUES.

1676 A Miniature of Agnes Rubens.
*A beautiful little work, on silver.*

1677 Portrait of Le Connetable de Bourbon, represented in profile, in a rich dress, with a cap and feather.

### LUINI, (AFTER).

1678 The Virgin and Child.

### SCHIDONE.

1679 The Girl with the Horn Book.

*The well known picture, formerly in the Palace of Capo di Monti, Naples.*

## GUIDO RENI.

1680 Lucretia.

*Very sweetly and delicately painted. The pearly tone of the flesh has a charming effect.*

## SPAGNOLETTO.

1681 St. Jerome awoke from his meditations by an Angel.

*A noble gallery picture. This subject is etched by the artist.*

## S. DEL PIOMBO.

1682 Lovers' Quarrels; said to be portraits of Raffaelle and La Fornarina.

## L. DA CREDI.

1683 The Holy Family—circular.

## TENIERS.

1684 Melchisedec bringing Bread and Wine to Abraham, on his return from the Slaughter of the Chedarlaomer.

*A pasticcio in the manner of Rubens.*

## BAGNACAVALLO.

1685 Holy Family with St. Philip and St. Anthony, and St. Sebastian. In the foreground is the Virgin, seated on a block of stone, in front of a column; the Infant Christ is on her lap, and bends forward to caress the little St. John, who kneels by the side of the Virgin; to the left of the picture are St. Anthony, and St. Philip with his Cross—on the right, St. Joseph, and St. Sebastian pierced with arrows; above is a choir of singing Angels. *From Mr. Solly's collection.*

## VELASQUEZ.

1686 Lot and his Daughters. Lot and his daughters are represented at the entrance of the cave in which, on their flight into Zoar, they are recorded to have dwelt. The patriarch is asleep, his head resting in his daughter's lap. There is a fine expression of mingled wonder and alarm in the countenance of the daughter, who appears pointing to some object in the distant landscape.

*A large gallery picture, boldly and vigorously treated. Formerly in the Orleans Gallery.*

## GIORGIONE.

1687 The Woman taken in Adultery. The incident described being that spoken of in John viii. 3.—" And the Scribes and Pharisees brought unto him a woman taken in adultery."

*A very richly toned and carefully finished picture.*

## P. P. RUBENS.

1688 A Lion Hunt. The composition consists of four huntsmen, mounted on fiery coursers, attacking a lion and lioness. In the conflict, one of the horses has fallen and pitched its rider headforemost to the ground, and an enraged lion has seized him on the back with its fore paws, and at the same instant has fixed the claws of one of its hinder feet in the face of a prostrate horseman, who is plunging a sword into the animal's belly.

*Engraved by Soutman and Le Bas. Smith's catalogue, p.* 274, *No.* 926.

## A. ALLORI.

1689 St. John in the Desert.

## DAVID TENIERS.

1690 The Alchymist. The interior of a Chemist's Laboratory. The operator is standing at a furnace watching the result of some experiment; three of his assistants busily engaged are at a furnace in another part of the room; they are overlooked by a man from a little window above; numerous alembics, retorts, crucibles, books, &c. are distributed in every part of the room; a spaniel lies asleep in front.

*Smith's Catalogue, No.* 520, *page* 398.

## GUERCINO.

1691 Samson and the Honeycomb.

*The celebrated chef-d'œuvre which once adorned the Grand Saloon of the Colonna Palace at Rome.*

## GUERCINO.

1692 Christ and the Woman of Samaria—companion to the preceding picture.

*From the Balbi Palace, and Sir Simon Clarke's collection.*

## LUDOVICO CARACCI.

1693 Cleopatra.

*Soft and transparent in the colouring, and the drawing excellent.*

## GIORGIONE.

1694 A Musical Party. The group is composed of a young man playing on a musical instrument, and two females seated on the ground in a landscape, adorned with buildings and a lake.

*A very fine picture of the Venetian School; painted with great breadth, and with that deep toned brightness for which the masters of that school were so famous.*

## CARLO DOLCI.

1695 St. John. The surprising beauty of this admirable work, whether for colouring, breadth of effect, or exquisite finish, renders all eulogy superfluous. The most accomplished connoisseur, and the most superficial lover of the art, would be alike attracted by it. The Apostle is represented as in the act of writing the Apocalypse.

*From the Lucien Bonaparte Gallery, afterwards in the collection of Sir Simon Clarke.*

## BENVENUTO GAROFALO.

1696 The Stoning of St. Stephen. The Saint is represented kneeling, with an expression of countenance mild and full of resignation, and finely contrasted with the savage and furious zeal of his persecutors. A vision of the Saviour and the Father surrounded by Angels, appears in the clouds. "But he being full of the Holy Ghost, looked up steadfastly into heaven, and saw the glory of God, and Jesus standing on the right hand of God.—Acts vii., 55.

*This magnificent work formerly adorned the Balbi Palace, and was brought to this country by that eminent collector Mr. Mawson.*

### C. DA SESTO.

1697 The Virgin, Infant Saviour, and St. John.

### GAROFALO.

1698 The Virgin and Infant Saviour.

### GUIDO.

1699 The Virgin with the Sleeping Infant.

## PICTURES FROM NORTHWICK PARK.

### BENEDETTO MONTAGNA.

1700 The Virgin Enthroned, with Saints.

*A grand gallery picture.*

### PALMA VECCHIO.

1701 The Virgin and Child, with Saint Catherine, and Saints kneeling in adoration.

### MARONI.

1702 Portrait of a Venetian Nobleman.

### JAN DE MABUSE.

1703 The Virgin with the Infant Saviour.

*A very elaborate and beautifully finished picture.*

### SIMONE DA PESARO.

1704 The Holy Family, with Angels worshipping.

### C. CIGNANI.

1705 The Virgin and Child and St. John.

### F. WILKIN.

1706 The Holy Family, after Raffaelle. *A fine drawing.*

### SOLEMACKER.

1707 An upright Landscape, with a group of cattle and figures in the foreground.

### P. DE HOOGHE.

1708 Interior of an Apartment, with figures, ladies at work.

## LORENZO DE CREDI.

1709 The Virgin with the Infant Saviour.

*A beautiful cabinet specimen.*

... ... ...

1710 Portrait of Columbus.

## P. P. RUBENS.

1711 Christ delivering the Keys of Heaven to St. Peter, in the presence of four other Disciples. The Saviour is represented with his left hand raised above his head, and Peter while receiving the keys looks up in his master's face. The figures are life size.

*This fine work was painted for the chapel of the tomb of John Breughel and his family, in the church of Notre Dame de la Chapelle, at Brussels, from whence it was sold in* 1765, *to defray the expenses of repairing the church, to M. Braamcamp, it afterwards become the property of M. Van Lankeren of Antwerp, at the sale of whose effects in* 1833 *it was purchased by the late Noble Owner.*

## BELLINI.

1712 The Prophet Ezra delivering to the Persian Governor of Judea the Commission of Axtaxerxes for the rebuilding of the Temple. *From the collection of R. Westall, Esq.*

## LUCAS KRANACK.

1713 Portrait of the Emperor Maximilian.

## GREUZE.

1714 Two Children at a Window.

## GIORGIONE.

1715 The Virgin and Child, with St. Francis.

*From the collection of R. Westall, Esq.*

## ANDREA DEL SARTO.

1716 Charity—Figures of life size.

*Signed and dated* 1536. *From the collection of Joseph Bonaparte.*

## E. VANDER NEER.

1717 Interior of an Apartment, with a Lady at her Toilet, a Cavalier entering.

## A. FRASER.

1718 Portrait of a Lady, bearing a dish of fruit.

## ANDREA VERONICA.

1719 The Wise Mens' Offering.

## VENUSTI.

1720 The Holy Family, with the Sleeping Infant.

## PORBUS.

1721 Portrait of Sir Francis Walsingham.

## S. BOURDON.

1722 A Roman Sacrifice.

## SCHALCKEN.

1723 Children blowing Bubbles by Candlelight.

## RAFFAELLE SCHOOL.

1724 The Holy Family.

## VILLAVICENZIO.

1725 The Holy Family with Angels.

## MABUSE.

1726 Portrait of Philip le Bel, son of the Emperor Maximilian.

## VAN EYCK (SCHOOL).

1727 Portrait of a Man in a black cap and a crimson dress.

## L. PENNI.

1728 The Holy Family.

## BASSANO.

1729 The Mocking of Christ.

### RAFFAELLE (SCHOOL).

1730 The Vision of Ezekiel.

### CANTARINI.

1731 The Coronation of the Virgin.

### C. REEPEL.

1732 A Group of Fruit on a marble slab. *Very highly finished.*

... ... ...

1733 Portrait of W. Shippen, Esq., M.P. for Newton.

### ALESSANDRO VERONESE.

1734 Dead Christ with the Maries.

### S. ROSA.

1735 A Grand Battle Piece, with numerous figures. *Very spirited.*

### S. ROSA.

1736 The Companion Picture.

### SASSO FERRATO (AFTER).

1737 A Magdalen.

### REINAGLE (AFTER HOBBIMA).

1738 A Wooded Landscape with figures.

### KOBEL.

1730 A Cow in a Landscape.

### CARACCI (STYLE OF).

1740 The Holy Family.

### DENIS.

1741 View near Naples.

### KEISERMAN.

1742 A Pair of Landscapes, in water colours.

R. WESTALL.

1743 A Girl at a Well—a drawing.

MURILLO (AFTER).

1744 The Nativity—a drawing.

BEATTIE, (AFTER DANBY).

1745 The Wood Nymph's Song.

BEATTIE, (AFTER VERNET).

1746 A Sea Port in the Levant.

ALBANO.

1747 The Saviour and Mary Magdalen.

CARACCI (AFTER).

1748 Christ bearing his Cross.

TIEPOLO.

1749 A Sketch.

---

A. A 10 ft. 6 mahogany frame Picture Easel, on castors, brass handles, lined with crimson cloth.

B. A 9 ft. ditto ditto.

C. A 9 ft. ditto ditto.

D. A 13 ft. ditto ditto.

E. A 7 ft. ditto, with double sides, lined with crimson cloth.

F. A ditto ditto.

*End of the Seventeenth Day's Sale.* £10,774.

# EIGHTEENTH DAY'S SALE.

On WEDNESDAY, the 24th day of AUGUST, 1859.

AT ONE O'CLOCK PRECISELY.

## PICTURES FROM NORTHWICK PARK.

A DEL SARTO (SCHOOL OF).

1750 The Virgin and Child.

MURILLO.

1751 The Virgin and Child.

MIGNARD.

1752 The Nativity.

BASSANO.

1753 Christ in the Garden of Gethsemane.

MABUSE.

1754 The Virgin and Child.

BAROCCIO.

1755 Portrait of the Artist.

HANDEROY.

1756 The Pool of Bethesda.

P. VERONESE.

1757 Portrait of a Doge of Venice.

### MURILLO.

1758 The Virgin with the Infant Saviour.
*From the Collection of Joseph Bonaparte.*

### CARLO CIGNANI.

1759 Portrait of Pope Pius V.

### GREEK SCHOOL.

1760 The Virgin and Child.

### S. DEL PIOMBO.

1761 Saint Dominic. *From the Lucca Gallery.*

### J. VAN LEYDEN.

1762 Portrait of a Man.

### VELASQUEZ.

1763 Portrait of a Gentleman in a ruff.

### F. ANGELL.

1764 Portrait of Lord Goring.

### MANTEGNA.

1765 Holy Family and St. John.—*Engraved by Marc Antonio.*

### FRADELLE.

1766 Abelard and Heloise.

### GLOVER.

1767 A Landscape, with cattle and figures.

### S. ROSA.

1768 A Rocky Scene, with figures.

### OLD BREUGHEL.

1769 A Village Fête, with numerous figures, Antwerp in the distance.

### PORDENONE.

1770 Christ curing the Blind.

## GHISOLPHI.

1771 A Landscape, with ruins and figures.

## CANALETTO.

1772 Scene on the Canal, Venice.

## CARACCI (SCHOOL).

1773 The Reposo in a landscape.

## JEROME FRANCKS.

1774 The Crucifixion.

## VENETIAN SCHOOL.

1775 St. Jerome at prayer in a landscape.

## DOMENICHINO.

1776 A grand Landscape, with Christ journeying to Emmaus.
*From the Jiustiniani Palace at Rome.*

## ELSHEIMER.

1777 The Flight into Egypt.

## MARIESCHI.

1778 The Doge's Palace at Venice.

## C. JANSENS.

1779 Elizabeth, Queen of Bohemia.

## W. HAVELL.

1780 The Terrace of the Convent of the Capucins at Sorrento.

## FIESOLE.

1781 A Female Saint.

## ALBANO.

1782 A grand Landscape, with the Death of Adonis.

## GUERCINO (COPY).

1783 Christ and the Woman of Samaria.

Y

DOMENICHINO.

1784 Timocles brought before Alexander.

C. POELEMBURG.

1785 A grand Landscape, with Nymphs and Satyrs dancing.
*An important work. From the collection of the Chevalier Erard.*

MIGNARD.

1786 Portrait of the Countess of Soissons, Mother of Prince Eugene of Savoy.

BISCAINO.

1787 The Nativity.

GABRIELLI RUSTICI.

1788 Head of Christ.

DIETRICY.

1789 Nymphs and Shepherds with cattle, in a Landscape.—*Engraved.*

PAUL BRILL.

1790 A Rocky Landscape, with Waterfall and Nymphs.

G. NETSCHER.

1791 Portrait of a Princess of the House of Orange, with a Dog.

LUINI.

1792 St. John.

MIGNARD (AFTER RAFFAELLE).

1793 The Holy Family.

P. P. RUBENS.

1794 A Man tuning a Guitar.
*A brilliantly coloured and vigorous portrait.*

VANDYCK (SCHOOL).

1795 Portrait of Snyders.

FIESOLE (SCHOOL).

1796 The Virgin and Child.

### L. CORNELITZ.

1797 Portrait of a Lady in a rich costume.

### COREGGIO (AFTER).

1798 The Virgin and Child.

### EDMONSTONE.

1799 A Girl Knitting—a sketch.

### HOLBEIN (SCHOOL).

1800 Portrait of the Earl of Surrey.

### GUERCINO.

1801 The Virgin with the Infant Saviour.

### A. FRASER.

1802 The Antiquary. *An important work.*

### C. JANSEN.

1803 Portrait of the Earl of Caernarvon.

### VELASQUEZ.

1804 Portrait of the Duke Olivarez.

### G. CUYP.

1805 Portrait of a Dutch Burgomaster.

### ZOUST.

1806 Portrait of the Duke of Monmouth.

### A DEL SARTO (SCHOOL).

1807 A Female Saint.

### BAROCCIO.

1808 The Holy Family with Angels.

### NICCOLO POUSSIN.

1809 A Landscape, with Nymphs and Satyrs.

### SEBASTIANO GOMEZ.

1810 The Annunciation.

## L. DE HEERE.

1811 Portrait of a Lady, in a fancy costume, and hat and feathers.

## VAN ASSELYN.

1812 A Sea Port, with figures.

## GAINSBOROUGH.

1813 Portrait of William Pitt when young—half length.

## RUBENS (AFTER).

1814 Mars and Venus—a sketch.

## G. POUSSIN.

1815 A Classical Landscape and figures.

## VANDERNEER.

1816 A Landscape, with wooded scenery and a marsh—moonlight.

## CUYP.

1817 A River Scene, with cattle and figures.

## GUERCINO.

1818 Mary Magdalen, half length.

*From the Gallery of Lucien Bonaparte.*

## BRONZINO.

1819 Portrait of a Nobleman in a black dress.

## ANNIBALE CARACCI.

1820 A Sleeping Nymph and a Satyr.

## GASPAR DE CRAYER.

1821 Christ delivering the Keys to Peter.

## GREEK SCHOOL.

1822 The Crucifixion.

## ARTHOIS.

1823 A Landscape, with figures by D. TENIERS.

BOGDANI.

1824 A Group of Fruit, with a Parrot.

TILBURGH.

1825 Interior—Peasants at a Repast.

MICHAEL CARRÉ.

1826 A Landscape with cattle.

JAN STEEN.

1827 An Interior—Boors Regaling.

G. POUSSIN.

1828 An Italian Landscape and figures.

N. POUSSIN.

1829 A Landscape, with shepherds and goats.

SWANEVELDT.

1830 An Italian Landscape, with figures.

GUERCINO.

1831 Endymion Asleep, half length.

*From the Gallery of Lucien Bonaparte.*

PILLEMANS.

1832 A Landscape, with cattle and figures.

SIR J. REYNOLDS (AFTER).

1833 Portrait of a Lady.

PATEL.

1834 A Landscape, with figures shearing sheep.

SIR J. REYNOLDS.

1835 The Flight into Egypt.

JAN WYNANTS.

1836 A View of the Exterior of a Chateau, with numerous cattle and figures introduced by LINGLEBACK.

CARAVAGGIO.

1837 Head of a Warrior.

FRA BARTOLOMEO.

1838 The Virgin and Child and St. John.

R. WESTALL.

1839 The Death of the Virgin.

GUIDO.

1840 The Magdalen.

A. KAUFFMAN.

1841 A Scene from Tasso, a sketch.

CANTARINI.

1842 Holy Family with St. John.

ROMANELLI.

1843 Charity.

... ... ...

1844 Portrait of Berardi.

BASSANO.

1845 The Angel appearing to the Shepherds.

ARTOIS.

1846 A grand Landscape, with figures.

GONZALES COQUES.

1847 Portrait of the Artist and his Wife—a pair, miniatures.

VANDERWERF

1848 Portrait of La Fontaine.

CANALETTO (Copy).

1849 A Scene in Venice.

EARLY FLORENTINE.

1850 The Virgin and Child.

GIOTTO.

1851 Saint Ambrose.

GREEK SCHOOL.

1852 The Virgin and Child.

GREEK SCHOOL.

1853 The Virgin and Child, with Saints.

F. MOLA.

1854 A Sybil.

RUBENS (SCHOOL).

1855 The Holy Family.

VELASQUEZ.

1856 A Landscape, with river scenery, and numerous figures.

GIORGIONE (SCHOOL).

1857 The Holy Family.

A. DEL SARTO (Copy).

1858 The Virgin Child, and St. John.

A. FRASER.

1859 Interior of a Highland Cottage.

A. DEL SARTO (Copy).

1860 The Virgin and Child, and St. Francis,

LORENZO MONACCO.

1861 The Virgin and Child, and Saints—a triptic.

RUBENS (Copy).

1862 The Marriage of St. Catherine.

GREEK SCHOOL.

1863 Virgin and Child, with Saints.

F. PORBUS.

1864 Portrait of a Lady of Distinction.

MARGARITONE.

1865 The Virgin and Child.

MAAS.

1866 The Shepherd's Offering.

SWANEVELDT.

1867 A Landscape, with the Flight into Egypt.

BECCAFUME.

1868 The Annunciation.

DE HEUISCH.

1869 An Italian Scene, with cattle and figures.

... ... ...

1870 Portrait of Voltaire.

ROMNEY.

1871 Study of two Female Heads—L'Allegro e il Penseroso.

MURILLO (AFTER).

1872 The Assumption of the Virgin.

PARMEGIANO.

1873 The Holy Family.

HERBERT, R.A.

1874 Marguerite.

PASSMORE.

1875 An Affecting Story.

ZURBARAN.

1876 St. Philip.

SCHIAVONE.

1877 Bathsheba at the Bath.

S. ROSA.

1878 A rocky Landscape, with figures.

## S. ROSA.

1879 The Companion Picture.

## OLD STONE.

1880 Portrait of Charles I. in his robes, small whole length.

## POLIDORO.

1881 Cupids Sporting.

# PICTURE EASELS, CASES, &c.

1882 A handsome 6 ft. *Spanish mahogany Picture Case,* on carved standards, enclosed by folding doors, lined with blue cloth.

1883 A ditto, with double sides, 7 ft. long and 6 ft. high, brass castors and handles, lined with crimson cloth.

1884 A ditto ditto, similar.

1885 A 4 ft. 3 ditto.

1886 A 3 ft. 9 ditto.

1887 A ditto ditto.

1888 A 2 ft. 9 ditto.

1889 A ditto, 8 ft. 6 high, 4 ft. 6 wide, and 8½ inches deep.

1890 A mahogany frame double Picture Easel, on castors, lined with crimson cloth.

1891 A pair of ditto ditto

1892 A pair of 2 ft. 6 ditto ditto

1893 Two ditto, 3 ft. and 2 ft. 4

1894 Two ditto, 6 ft. and 4 ft.

*End of the Eighteenth Day's Sale.*

# THE FURNITURE, PLATE, WINES,

AND EFFECTS,

## AT THIRLESTANE HOUSE,

CHELTENHAM.

# NINETEENTH DAY'S SALE.

On THURSDAY, the 25th day of AUGUST, 1859,

AT ONE O'CLOCK PRECISELY.

## UPPER CHAMBERS.

LOT

1 A mahogany leg-rest, covered in morocco, and two chairs, fancy seats.

2 Painted French bedstead, 2 straw palliasses, 2 chairs, and a painted dressing-table.

3 A birch French bedstead, palliasse, three chairs, and a painted table.

4 A 4 ft. 3 in. French bedstead, brass pole, and drab moreen curtains, palliasse, wool mattress, and a feather bed.

5 A feather bed, bolster, 3 blankets, and a coverlid.

6 A painted washstand, white fittings, dressing table, 2 chairs, and a leg-rest.

7 A mahogany commode front chest of 5 drawers.

8 A toilet glass in mahogany frame, on scroll supports, plate 20 by 17.

9 A steel fender, set of fire irons, 2 wire fire guards, and a slop pail.

10 A deal table, fender with standards, and 2 brass wire fire guards.

11 A turks head broom, polishing brush, and various brooms.

12 An ornamented wine cooler, japanned with copper liner.

13 An oval mahogany wine cooler, brass bound and lined, and a japanned plate warmer.

14 A birch French bedstead, and a painted chest of drawers.

15 A ditto, ditto, painted washstand, rush seat chair, tin foot bath, and a leg rest.

16 Four rosewood frame chairs, stuffed seats, covered in tabaret.

17 Two ditto easy chairs to match.

18 A ditto sofa, thickly stuffed, and loose pillows to match.

## NORTH CHAMBER.

19 A drab ground Brussels carpet, 20 ft. by 14, fender and a set of fire irons.

20 A 6 ft. SPANISH MAHOGANY FOUR-POST BEDSTEAD, fitted with patent springs, moulded cornice, chintz furniture lined.

21 Two pairs of chintz window curtains to match bed furniture, and moulded cornices.

22 A straw palliasse, and a thick wool mattress, in holland case, to fit the bedstead.

23 Feather bolster, and 2 down pillows.

24 Three large blankets, and a white Marseilles quilt.

25 A mahogany folding towel horse, & 3 painted chairs with rush seats.

26 A Spanish mahogany table, with 2 flaps and drawer, hearth brush, pincushion, watch stand, kettle holder, match pot, and a blotting book.

27 A 4 ft. painted tray top washstand, two drawers, and a ditto dressing table, two drawers.

28 A set of drab and white toilet fittings, consisting of ewer and basin, smaller ditto, sponge tray, brush tray, pomade pot, soap tray, slop pail, foot bath, large water jug, pair of high candlesticks, flat candlestick, and a chamber water bottle and tumbler.

29 A Spanish mahogany chest of 5 drawers.

30 A mahogany double rail towel horse, and a footstool covered with carpet.

31 A Spanish mahogany frame swing toilet glass, plate 21 by 18.

32 A handsome 3 ft. rosewood pedestal nest of drawers, fitted with secretaire, enclosed by one lock.

33 A capital 4 ft. 6 mahogany wardrobe, fitted with four drawers, the upper part enclosed by 2 panel doors, arranged with five trays.

34 A rosewood frame easy chair on castors, spring stuffed seat, covered with striped linen, and extra dimity cover.

35 A Spanish mahogany bedside cupboard, tray top.

## DRESSING ROOM.

36 A folding chair bedstead, covered with striped linen, and three hair cushions.

37 Feather bed and pillow, 3 blankets, and a coverlid.

38 A painted dressing table, with drawer, a toilet glass in mahogany frame and fittings.

39 A mahogany portable water closet, complete.

40 An 8 ft. painted deal dwarf bookcase, fitted with shelves.

## WEST CHAMBER.

41 A drab and crimson Brussels carpet as planned, measuring 22 ft. by 20 ft., and a hearth rug.

42 High wire fender, brass mounted, set of fire irons, and copper coal scuttle.

43 A chimney glass, in a neat ornamented gilt frame, plate 42 by 28.

44 A HANDSOME 6 ft. EBONY BEDSTEAD, WITH RICHLY CARVED PILLARS, fitted with patent springs, gilt cornice, and drab figured damask furniture.

45 A thick wool mattrass to fit in a holland case.

46 A capital large goose feather bed.

47 A ditto bolster, 2 pillows, and a blanket.

48 Two large blankets, and a white Marseilles quilt.

49 Two pairs of drab damask window curtains, to match bed furniture; holders and draperies, and the two 6 ft. 6 gilt cornices with return ends.

50 Five birch frame chairs, cane seats, and a footstool covered in carpet.

51 A mahogany bedside cupboard, marble slab, tray top, and a double rail towel horse.

52 A 4 ft. painted tray top washstand, 2 drawers, and a set of neat flowered pattern fittings, consisting of ewer and basin, smaller ditto, sponge basin, brush tray, soap dish, covered jug, toilet box, foot pan, slop pail, large water jug, pair of high candlesticks, pair of chamber ditto, 2 chambers, and a water bottle and tumbler.

53 A HANDSOME SPANISH MAHOGANY FRAME TOILET GLASS, on column supports, fitted with 2 drawers, plate, 24 in. 18.

54 An EXCELLENT CARVED SPANISH MAHOGANY FRAME EASY CHAIR, on castors, spring stuffed seat, covered in crimson morocco.

55 A Spanish mahogany pembroke table, fitted with drawer.

56 A HANDSOME 6 FT. SPANISH MAHOGANY WARDROBE, moulded cornice, enclosed by 3 doors, the interior fitted with trays, drawers, and hanging pegs.

57 A DITTO DITTO CHEVAL GLASS, on pillar supports, plate 44 by 24.

58 A 4 ft. 6 painted deal dressing table, 2 drawers, and a footstool covered in carpet.

59 A walnut frame easy chair on castors, cane back and seats.

60 A 4 ft. 6 deal painted toilet table, 2 drawers, and a mahogany bed-side cupboard, marble slab, tray top.

61 A capital Spanish mahogany chest of 5 drawers.

## DRESSING ROOM.

62 A high wire fender, brass mounted, set of fire irons, hearth brush, and a footstool covered with carpet.

63 The drab ground Brussels carpet, as planned, 14 ft. by 11, and a hearth rug.

64 A HANDSOME 3 ft. 9 SPANISH MAHOGANY FRENCH BEDSTEAD, on French castors, lath bottom, canopy top, expensive furniture, and a palliasse to fit.

65 A thick wool mattrass in linen case.

66 A capital feather bed, bolster and pillow.

67 Three blankets and a counterpane.

68 A 4 ft. 6 painted deal dressing table, a ditto wash stand, tray top, blue and white fittings, water bottle and tumbler.

69 Two birch frame chairs, cane seats, a Spanish bed-side cupboard, and a towel horse.

70 A 3 ft. Spanish mahogany chest of 4 drawers.

71 A pair of drab moreen window curtains, fringe draperies and holders, moulded mahogany cornice.

72 A SPANISH MAHOGANY FRAME TOILET GLASS, on carved columns, fitted with 2 drawers, plate 24 by 18.

73

## MODERN GALLERY.

74 THE HANDSOME CRIMSON GROUND BRUSSELS CARPET, as planned to room, 40 ft. by 23 ft.

75 A HANDSOME 5 ft. 9 SPANISH MAHOGANY TABLE, fitted for books, with sliding trays on castors, enriched with gilt mouldings, top covered in crimson cloth.

76 A 7 ft. 6. CENTRE SETTEE of elegant design, thickly stuffed, and covered in crimson Utrecht velvet

77 A HANDSOME 4 FT. WALNUT WOOD CENTRE SALOON TABLE, THE TOP INLAID WITH THE FAMILY ARMS, on a richly carved pillar and claw.

## VENETIAN ROOM.

78 Six rosewood frame chairs, 2 having arms, fancy rush seats, and 2 footstools, covered in chintz.

79 A circular rosewood frame sofa, stuffed spring seats, and covered in crimson Utrecht velvet.

80 A ditto ditto, the companion.

81 A grand piano forte, in a mahogany case, by Mott.

82 A pair of 3 ft. 9 enclosed mahogany bookcases, inlaid with various woods, fitted with numerous shelves.

83 A BEAUTIFUL NEEDLEWORK SCREEN, mounted on a richly carved and gilt stand.

84 A 16 ft. brass curtain pole with rings, and 2 carved eagles at the ends.

85 A rosewood vis à vis couch, stuffed seat, covered in crimson damask

86 The bordered crimson ground Brussels carpet, as planned to the room, 30 ft. by 24 ft.

## LANDSCAPE GALLERY,

87 A handsome polished steel fender, and a set of fire irons.

88 A BEAUTIFUL AUBUSSON CARPET, bordered, and worked in scrolls, 30 ft. by 23 ft.

89 Four occasional chairs, stuffed seats, covered in crimson Utrecht velvet, and a pair of rosewood pole fire screens.

90 A ball frame rosewood vis-a-vis couch, stuffed seat, and top covered in striped crimson damask.

91 A thermometer, foot stool, covered in needlework, and a hearth brush.

92 A 4 ft. rosewood loo table, on carved pillar and claw.

93 A pair of ditto card tables to match, lined with crimson cloth.

94 A pair of 2 ft. 3. mahogany bookstands, fitted with drawers, gilt enrichments.

95 A handsome 4 ft. 6. walnut wood loo table, the top inlaid in Marqueterie, on carved pillar and claw.

96 A 4 ft. stained loo table, and 18 yds. of Brussels carpet.

## CABINET ROOM.

97 The bordered Brussels carpet, crimson ground, as planned, 24 ft. by 18
98 Eight carved frame rosewood chairs, stuffed seats, covered in Utrecht velvet.
99 A pair of pier glasses, in gilt frames.
100 Two occasional chairs, seats stuffed and covered, and a deal bookcase.
101 A handsome walnut wood Davenport, fitted with numerous drawers, gallery top, covered in leather.
102 A pair of 2 ft. mahogany book stands, or-molu mounted, fitted with 3 drawers each.
103 A 7 ft. centre ottoman, thickly stuffed, and covered in crimson damask.
104 A pair of papier machée bellows, 2 magnifying glasses, 2 thermometers, and 2 picture glasses.
105 A 3 ft. mahogany bookcase, gilt mouldings, and a book stand.
106 A handsome papier machée coffee table—subject after Landseer.

## DINING ROOM.

107 A handsome steel fender, with standards, set of fire irons, and a small mahogany table.
108 A crimson Brussels carpet, planned to room, 32 ft. by 23 ft.
109 A CAPITAL 10 ft. 3. SPANISH MAHOGANY SIDEBOARD, on carved legs, fitted with 2 drawers.
110 EIGHTEEN DITTO DINING ROOM CHAIRS, stuffed seats and backs, covered in crimson in Utrecht velvet, at per chair.
111 A set of SPANISH MAHOGANY DINING TABLES, in parts, extending 18 ft. by 5 ft. 6.
112 A PAIR of DITTO FIRE SCREENS, with 3 leaves, ruled joints, covered in crimson damask.
113 Two pairs of rich crimson damask window curtains, brass pole, 31 ft. long, rings, ends, and ornaments complete.
114 A mahogany paper and envelope case, expensively fitted.

## PARLOUR.

115 A polished steel fender, with standards, and a set of fire irons, and 2 hearth brushes.
116 The crimson ground Brussels carpet, planned to room, 21 ft. by 16 ft.

117 A pair of drab tabaret window curtains, brass pole, 20 ft. long, rings, holders, &c. complete.

118 Six stained frame chairs, cane backs and seats, loose cushions covered in crimson damask.

119 A large sofa, thickly stuffed, 3 loose squabs, covered in drab tabaret.

120 A mahogany frame easy chair, cane back and seat, loose cushions, covered in crimson cloth.

121 A handsome rosewood centre table, satin wood border, inlaid with brass.

122 A 4 ft. mahogany bookcase, fitted with secretaire, with glazed folding doors.

123 A glass in mahogany frame.

124 A rosewood Davenport, fitted with drawers, top covered in leather.

125 A rosewood case, with glass doors, 2 spill cases, 2 pen wipers envelope case, waste paper basket and a rosewood letter case.

126 A VERY EXPENSIVE ROSEWOOD PRINT CASE, 14 ft. by 3 ft. 6, richly carved and ornamented with gilt enrichments, enclosed by six doors filled with brass net-work.

127 Two 5 ft. mahogany hall benches and a 4 ft. table on carved legs

## LIBRARY.

128 A handsome polished steel fender, with standards, and a set of fire irons.

129 A crimson ground Brussels carpet, planned to room, 22 ft. square.

130 A brilliant plate chimney glass, in a rich gilt frame, carved ornamental top; the plate 76 by 54.

131 Four stained frame chairs, cane seats, loose stuffed seats, covered in crimson damask.

132 A ball frame rosewood double headed settee, hair and spring stuffed, covered in crimson Utrecht velvet.

133 A handsome 5 ft. rosewood loo table, on carved pillar and claw.

134 A pair of crimson and drab tabaret window curtains, trimmed with gimp, and holders fitted to brass pole, rings and ends complete.

135 A maple wood book stand, with drawers, and a foot-stool covered in needlework.

136 A HANDSOME AUBUSSON TABLE COVER, worked in gold.

## CIRCULAR ROOM.

137 A length of Brussels carpet, 30 ft. by 5 wide, and another 21 ft. by 4 ft. 6.

138 Four rosewood chairs, cane seats.

139 A HANDSOME OVAL SHAPE ROSEWOOD CENTRE TABLE, on carved pillar and claw.

140 A satin wood writing table, with drawers, top covered in leather, and a mahogany miniature case, gilt door.

141 A set of draftmen in ivory, and a similar set of wood.

142 Two 4 ft. mahogany tables, on carved legs.

## INNER HALL AND STAIRCASE.

143 The oil cloth as planned, 25 ft by 13.

144 About 60 yds. of 36 in. bordered Brussels stair carpet.

145 Thirty-six brass stair rods.

146 A pair of handsome table lamps, on twisted spiral ebony columns, marble base.

147 Two door porters, deal table, piece of drugget, and chair to form steps.

148 Housemaid's box, various brushes and brooms, dust pan, hammer, pincers and a screw driver, 2 door porters and a piece of carpet.

149 Two copper coal scuttles.

150 Three pieces of oil cloth, 2 patterns, piece of carpet, and 3 mats.

151 A pair of 10-tread painted steps.

*End of the Nineteenth Day's Sale.*

# TWENTIETH DAY'S SALE.

On FRIDAY, the 26th day of AUGUST, 1859,

AT ONE O'CLOCK PRECISELY.

## CHAMBER OVER SALOON.

LOT

152 The brown and white Brussels carpet as planned, about 35 yards, and a hearth rug to match, fringed.

153 A pierced fender, steel mounted; hearth brush, and a stool covered carpet.

154 A handsome 6 ft. Spanish mahogany 4-post Bedstead, moulded cornice and expensive chintz furniture, fringe trimmings, and a palliasse to fit.

155 A capital feather bed, bolster, and 2 pillows.

156 Three large blankets, and a Marseilles quilt.

157 Birch frame easy chair, spring stuffed, covered in striped cotton, and a bedside cupboard, marble slab, tray top.

158 Two pairs of chintz window curtains and draperies, moulded cornices, to match the bedstead.

159 Four birch frame chairs, cane seats, and a mahogany bedside cupboard, marble slab, tray top.

160 Mahogany towel horse, and a 5 ft. deal dressing table, 2 drawers.

161 A rosewood frame easy chair on castors, cane back and seat.

162 A deep seat birch frame arm chair, cane seat.

163 A handsome Spanish mahogany frame toilet glass, on richly carved standards, moulded base, plate 30 ft. by 20.

164 A 4 ft. 6 Spanish mahogany wardrobe, fitted with 4 drawers and 4 trays, the upper part enclosed by 2 panel doors.

165 A curious chimney glass, in compartments of Vauxhall plates, in a gilt frame.

166 A pair of pole fire screens, with drawings.

167 A 4 ft. painted wash stand, with 2 drawers, and a set of toilette fittings, viz., ewer and basin, sponge tray, soap and brush tray, foot bath, large water jug, slop pail, candlestick, water bottle and tumbler.

168 A HANDSOME CHEVAL DRESSING GLASS, on solid pillar supports and base, of choice Spanish mahogany, plate 44 by 24.

## DRESSING ROOM.

169 A drab and brown Brussels carpet, hearth rug, high wire fender, brass mounted, set of fire irons.

170 A HANDSOME 4 ft. SPANISH MAHOGANY FRENCH BEDSTEAD, on castors, tent cornice and expensive chintz furniture lined, and a palliasse to fit.

171 Wool mattrass in a linen case, bolster, and a pillow.

172 Feather bed, 3 blankets, and a quilt.

173 A mahogany bed-side cupboard and a boot and shoe horse.

174 Three birch chairs, cane seats, a painted wash stand, 2 drawers, blue and white fittings, water bottle and a tumbler.

175 A handsome Spanish mahogany chest of 5 drawers.

176 A 5 ft. deal dressing table, 2 drawers, mahogany towel horse, stool covered with carpet, and a pair of chintz window curtains, mahogany cornice.

177 A toilette glass, on carved Spanish mahogany column supports and base, plate 24 by 20.

## CHAMBER OVER DINING ROOM.

178 The Venetian carpet as planned, hearth rug, high wire fender, and set of fire irons.

179 A HANDSOME 6 ft. SPANISH MAHOGANY 4-POST BEDSTEAD, richly carved pillars, gilt cornice, French castors, expensive chintz furniture, lined and trimmed with fringe, and a thick bordered palliasse to fit.

180 A thick Spanish wool mattress, in linen tick.

181 A capital large goose feather bed, in bordered tick.

182 A bolster, 2 pillows, and a blanket.

183 Two fine Witney blankets, and a Marseilles quilt.

184 AN EXCELLENT 6 ft. SPANISH MAHOGANY WARDROBE, fitted with 3 panel doors enclosing trays, drawers, and hanging pegs.

185 Two rosewood frame easy chairs, on castors, spring seats, stuffed and covered in crimson morocco

186 A 3 ft. 9 Spanish mahogany chest of 5 drawers.

187 Six birch frame chairs, cane seats, and a folding towel horse.

188 A handsome chimney glass, in a carved and gilt frame, plate 40 by 28.

189 A 5 ft. deal dressing table, 2 drawers, and a mahogany bedside cupboard, marble top, tray top.

190 A capital 4 ft. Spanish mahogany washstand, marble slab, fitted with 2 drawers.

191 A set of toilet fittings (flowered pattern), viz., ewer and basin, sponge, soap and brush trays, powder bag, solp pail, hot water jug, foot bath, large jug, 2 high candlestick, chamber ditto, small jug, and 2 chambers.

192 A mahogany folding towel horse, and a bedside table, marble slab, tray top.

193 A Spanish mahogany Pembroke table, with drawer, and a footstool covered with carpet

194 Two pairs of chintz window curtains, with draperies, carved and gilt cornices.

195 A HANDSOME CHEVAL GLASS, on massive pillar supports and base, of fine Spanish manogany, plate 40 by 24.

196 A mahogany double rail towel horse, a footstool covered with carpet, blotting book, and an inkstand.

197 A HANDSOME SPANISH MAHOGANY SWING DRESSING GLASS, on carved columns, marble base, plate 29 by 20.

## DRESSING ROOM.

198 Venetian carpet as planned, hearth rug, high wire fender, brass mounted, and a set of polished steel fire irons.

199 A 3 ft. 6 SPANISH MAHOGANY FRENCH BEDSTEAD, lath bottom, on castors, canopy fitted with expensive chintz furniture, and a bordered palliasse.

200 A wool mattress, in linen case, 3 blankets, and a counterpane.

200* A feather bed, bolster, and pillow.

201 Three birch chairs, cane seats, and a mahogany bedside table, tray top.

202 A painted tray top wash stand, blue and white toilet fittings, water bottle and tumbler.

203 A 5 ft. painted dressing table, with 2 drawers, a footstool covered in carpet, and a towel horse.

204 A Spanish mahogany swing Toilet Glass, on carved pillar supports, fitted with 2 drawers in base, plate 24 by 20.

205 A pair of chintz window curtains, mahogany cornice, 2 match pots, and a taper candlestick.

206 A 3 ft. 6 chest of 5 drawers, of choice Spanish mahogany.

## SALOON.

207 Eight rosewood chairs, stuffed seats, covered in crimson Utrecht velvet.

208 Two white and gold settees, stuffed backs and seats, loose bolster, covered in silk.

209 Two pairs of crimson tabaret curtains, with a brass pole 35 ft. long rings, ends, holders, &c. complete.

210 Two pier glasses in ornamental gilt frames, plates 60 by 26 inches,

211 A chimney glass in neat gilt frame, plate 56 by 38 inches.

212 A ditto ditto to match.

213 Two rosewood letter racks, 2 door porters, and a 4 ft. 6. bookcase.

214 A piece of crimson Brussels carpet 35 ft. by 4 ft. 8. and a ditto 24 ft. by 4 ft. 6.

## DRAWING ROOM.

215 Crimson ground Brussels carpet, as planned to room, 32 ft. by 22 ft.

216 Two pairs of crimson tabaret window curtains, fitted to a brass pole of 30 ft., ends, ornaments rings, holders, &c. complete.

217 Six imitation rosewood frame chairs, cane seats, loose cushions, covered in crimson damask.

## PRINCIPAL GALLERY.

218 The crimson ground bordered Brussels carpet, 80 ft. by 17 ft.

219 An ornamental steel and iron fender, with standards, and a set of mounted fire irons.

220 A carved frame rosewood couch, with end, stuffed and covered in crimson velvet

221 A ditto ditto to match.

222 Four rosewood chairs, fancy seats.

223 An ottoman seat needlework cushion, and 2 hearth brushes.

224 A chimney glass, in an ornamental gilt frame, plate 74 by 38.

225 A pair of oval shape card tables, on carved pillar and blocks, and claw feet, the tops lined with crimson cloth.

226 A 6 ft. MAHOGANY TABLE, fitted with 12 drawers, cupboards, and print shelves.

## GIOTTO ROOM.

227 The nearly new crimson ground Brussels carpet, as planned, 23 ft. by 19 ft.

228 A carved frame rosewood couch, stuffed and covered in crimson Utrecht velvet.

## PARTHENON ROOM.

229 Two lengths of crimson ground Brussels carpet, each 19 ft. long by 6 ft. 9 wide.

230 Two ditto ditto, 28 ft. by 6 ft. 9, and 11 ft. by 4 ft. 6.

231 A carved rosewood frame circular-shaped back sofa, stuffed and covered in crimson Utrecht velvet.

232 A ditto ditto to match

233 A FINE-TONED FINGER ORGAN, in grained maple case, gilt pipes, 12 stops.

233* Three Vauxhall plates, in gilt frames.

## TITIAN ROOM.

234 Crimson drugget, as planned, 24 ft. by 18 ft.

235 A rose-wood frame double-headed couch, stuffed and covered with crimson Utrecht velvet.

## ENTRANCE HALL.

236 Eight brass stair rods, 8 door mats, iron scraper, and a foot brush.

237 The oil cloth as planned, 25 ft. by 13 ft.

238 A handsome sexagon shaped brass hall lamp, shades, &c., complete, and a long chain.

239 Four stained hall chairs, with crest.
240 A mahogany hat and umbrella stand.
241 A barometer, in a mahogany case, by Dolland.
242 A flight of 16-tread painted steps.
243 A ditto of 10-tier, and a mahogany table with tray top.

## LINEN.

244 Four pairs of fine linen sheets.
245 Four pairs of ditto, coarser.
246 Three pairs of ditto, large size.
247 Three pairs of ditto
248 Five pairs of linen sheets.
249 Five pairs of ditto.
250 Five pairs of ditto.
251 Four pairs of ditto, and 10 pairs of pillow cases
252 Ten pairs of pillow cases and 6 damask toilet covers.
253 Nine diaper toilet covers, 12 diaper chamber towels and 6 pillow cases.
254 Twelve fine diaper chamber towels, and 24 others.
255 Two fine large damask table cloths, large size (nearly new).
256 Five damask table cloths.
257 Five ditto.
258 Five ditto and 15 dinner napkins.
259 Eight breakfast table cloths.
260 Seventeen damask dinner napkins.
261 Twelve ditto.
262 Twelve ditto and 12 breakfast napkins.
263 Twenty-four dinner napkins.
264 Four hall table cloths and 4 housekeeper's ditto.
265 Five table cloths and 3 others.
266 Three round towels, 4 kitchen table cloths, 4 rubbers, 2 dishing-up cloths and 25 glass cloths.
267 Six new fish cloths and 12 old ditto, 6 new pastry cloths and 14 old ditto, 25 glass cloths, 12 knitted d'oyleys and 12 coloured ditto.

## PLATED WARE.

268 Eight oval dish covers in sizes.
269 Eight ditto ditto.
270 Two butter coolers, with glass liners.
271 Two goblets on feet, gilt inside.
272 Two chamber candlesticks and extinguishers, with glass shades.
273 Eight knife rests and a coffee pot.
274 An egg stand with 6 cups and 6 spoons, gilt inside.
275 A plated tea kettle, with stand and lamp.
276 A soufflet dish, cover and liner.
277 Two large chamber candlesticks and extinguishers and glass shades.
278 A large venison dish, and a lamp and stand.
279 A coffee pot, stand and lamp.
280 A boat-shape cruet frame with 7 glasses, and a toast rack.
281 A pair of high candlesticks, and 3 chamber ditto with extinguishers.
282 Four wine lables and 4 decanter stands.
283 A pair of high candlesticks, with shifting branches.
284 An iron-bound oak chest, with locks and keys.
285 A handsome plated epergne, with branches, and cut glass dishes.

## PLATE, AT PER OUNCE.

286 Six oval-shaped sauce boats and covers with handles, and lion on top.
287 Six circular salts, with chased edges, and 6 spoons gilt inside.
288 A tea service, consisting of tea pot, sugar basin, and cream ewer.
289 A coffee pot and stand.
290 A pair of high table candlesticks.
291 A lemon strainer.
292 Two dozen plain table forks.
293 Two dozen and six ditto, to match.
294 One dozen dessert forks.
295 Eighteen table spoons.
296 Eighteen ditto.
297 Eighteen ditto dessert spoons.
298 Eighteen tea spoons.
299 A soup ladle, 2 sauce ladles, and 2 gravy spoons.
300 A soup ladle and 4 sauce ladles.

301 Two gravy spoons, 2 sauce ladles, and a salad fork.
302 Asparagus tongs and a marrow spoon.
303 Four wine lables and a mustard spoon.
304 Four vegetable dishes and covers, with lion handles.
305 Forty-eight silver handled table knives.
306 Twelve silver handled dessert knives and a pair of carvers.

## THE CELLAR OF WINES.

Bin 1,

307 Two dozen and 6, more or less, St. Peray.

Bin 2.

308 One dozen Tinta Madeira.

Bin 3.

309 Two dozen and 3, more or less, East India Madeira.

Bin 4.

310 Two dozen St. Peray.
311 Two dozen ditto ditto.
312 Two dozen ditto ditto, more or less.

Bin 5.

313 Two dozen and 8, more or less, Madeira.

Bin 6.

314 One dozen and 9, more or less, Red Hermitage.

Bin 7.

315 Two dozen St. Peray.
316 Two dozen ditto ditto.
317 Two dozen and 9 ditto ditto, more or less.

Bin 8.

318 Two dozen St. Peray.

Bin 9.

319 Three dozen Port.
320 Two dozen and 8 ditto ditto, more or less.

BIN 10.

321 Three dozen MALMSEY MADEIRA.
322 Two dozen and 11, more or less.

BIN 11.

323 Two dozen MALMSEY MADEIRA (Pints)
324 Two dozen ditto ditto.

BIN 12.

325 Two dozen MALAGA (Pints).
326 One dozen and 9 ditto ditto, more or less.

BIN 13.

327 Two dozen WEST INDIA MADEIRA.
328 Two dozen ditto ditto.
329 One dozen and 8 ditto ditto, more or less.

BIN 14.

330 Two dozen WEST INDIA MADEIRA.
331 Two dozen ditto ditto.
332 Two dozen ditto ditto, more or less.

BIN 15.

333 Two dozen HOCK.
334 Two dozen ditto ditto.
335 Two dozen ditto ditto.
336 Two dozen and 6 ditto ditto, more or less.

BIN 17.

337 Two dozen and 6, more or less, ST. PERAY.

BIN 18.

338 Two dozen and 10, more or less, CLARET.

BIN 19.

339 One dozen and 9, more or less, MADEIRA.
340 Six bottles CLARET, and 6 bottles BRANDY.

BIN 21.

341 Two dozen MOSELLE.
342 Two dozen ditto.

343 Two dozen MOSELLE.
344 Two dozen ditto.
345 Two dozen ditto.
346 Two dozen and 4, more or less.

BIN 23.

347 One dozen and 8, more or less, CHAMPAGNE.

BIN 24.

348 Two dozen and 11, more or less, CLARET.

BIN 25.

349 Two dozen and 11, more or less, ST. PERAY.

BIN 26.

350 Two dozen and 11, more or less, MOUSSEAU, S. P.

BIN 27.

351 Two dozen OLD MADEIRA.
352 Two dozen ditto ditto.
353 Two dozen ditto ditto.
354 Two dozen and 11 ditto, more or less.

BIN 28.

355 Two dozen MARSALA.
356 Two dozen ditto.
357 Two dozen ditto.
358 One dozen and 11 ditto, more or less.

BIN 29.

359 Two dozen LACHRYMA CHRISTI.
360 Two dozen ditto ditto.
361 Two dozen and 8 ditto ditto, more or less.

BIN 30.

362 Six bottles TOKAY, 4 bottles Lunelle, and 5 ditto **OLD RUM, more or less.**

BIN 31.

364 Two dozen of FINE OLD PORT.
365 Two dozen ditto.
366 Two dozen ditto.

367 Two dozen FINE OLD PORT.
368 Two dozen ditto.
369 Two dozen ditto.
370 Two dozen ditto.
371 Two dozen ditto.
372 Two dozen ditto.
373 Two dozen ditto.
374 Two dozen ditto.
374* Two dozen and 6 ditto, more or less.

BIN 33.

375 Two dozen and 6, more or less, OLD PORT.

BIN 34.

376 One dozen and 9, more or less, OLD HOCK.

BIN 37.

377 Two dozen and 2, more or less, RED HERMITAGE.

BIN 38.

378 One dozen and 2, more or less, WHITE HERMITAGE.

BIN 39

379 Two dozen CHAMPAGNE.
380 Two dozen and 2, more or less, BURGUNDY.

BIN 42.

381 One dozen and 3, more or less, LIGHT DINNER WINE.

BIN 43.

382 Ten bottles HOCK, and eleven ditto CLARET, more or less.

BIN 44.

383 Seven bottles of PORT, and 8 samples, more or less.

*End of the Twentieth Day's Sale.*

# TWENTY-FIRST DAY'S SALE.

On MONDAY, the 29th day of AUGUST, 1859,

AT ONE O'CLOCK PRECISELY.

## SOUTH CHAMBER.

LOT

384 The Venetian carpet as planned to room, hearth rug, high wire fender brass mounted, and a set of polished steel fire irons.

385 A 4 ft. 6 handsome Spanish mahogany French bedstead, on castors, canopy and expensive chintz furniture, and a palliasse to fit.

386 A thick wool mattress to fit.

387 A feather bed, bolster, and pillow.

388 Three blankets and a quilt.

389 Three painted chairs, cane seats, mahogany towel horse, leg rest, chair back, and a reading stand.

390 A mahogany bedside table, tray top, and an easy chair, spring, stuffed and covered in linen.

391 A japanned coal box and scoop, hearth brush, towel horse, and a footstool, covered in carpet.

392 A chimney glass, in a carved and gilt frame, plate 78 by 36.

393 A mahogany Pembroke table with drawer, and a bidet, white liner.

394 A painted tray top washstand, 2 drawers, and a 5 ft. dressing table, 2 drawers.

395 A Spanish mahogany commode front chest of 6 drawers.

396 Two pairs of chintz window curtains, lined, and 2 Spanish mahogany cornices.

397 A mahogany frame swing dressing glass, on scroll supports, plate 26 by 20.

## EAST CHAMBER.

398 The Venetian carpet as planned, 5 yards square, hearth rug, and carpeted footstool.

399 A pierced fender, set of polished steel fire irons, japanned coal scuttle and scoop, and a hearth brush.

400 A 4 FT. 6 SPANISH MAHOGANY FRENCH BEDSTEAD, scroll ends, canopy top, expensive chintz hangings, and palliasse to fit.

401 A thick wool mattress and linen case.

402 A feather bed, bolster, and pillow.

403 Three blankets and a Marseilles quilt.

404 A mahogany bedside cupboard, tray top, and 3 painted chairs, cane seats.

405 A rosewood chair, spring, stuffed and covered in striped cotton, and a mahogany towel horse.

406 A chimney glass, in a neat gilt frame, plate 78 by 36.

407 A painted tray top washstand, blue and white fittings, water bottle, and tumbler.

408 Three china candlesticks, match pot, blotting book, inkstand, and a folding mahogany towel horse.

409 A mahogany bidet, white liner, and a 5 ft. dressing table, with 2 drawers.

410 A 3 ft. 6 Spanish mahogany chest of 5 drawers.

411 Two pairs of chintz window curtains, lined, and 2 mahogany cornices.

412 A swing toilet glass, on scroll standards and base, plate 22 by 18.

413 A mahogany Pembroke table, with drawer.

## SOUTH EAST CHAMBER.

414 A tent bedstead, chintz furniture, and a hair mattrass.

415 A feather bed and bolster.

416 Three blankets and a coverlet.

417 A feather bed and pillow.

418 A swing toilet glass in mahogany frame, folding towel horse, wire fender, set of fire irons, hearth brush, and a piece of Brussels carpet, 14 ft. by 8.

419 A painted chest of 5 drawers and 3 chairs, rush seats.

420 A painted wash stand, blue and white fittings, and a toilet table with drawers.

## NORTH EAST CHAMBER.

421 A tent bedstead, chintz furniture and wool mattrass, 3 blankets and a coverlet.

422 A feather bed and bolster.

423 Mahogany frame swing glass, boot horse, 3 painted chairs, rush seats, and a towel horse.

424 A painted chest of 5 drawers, dressing table, 1 drawer, and a wash stand and part of fittings.

## SERVANT'S BED ROOM—No. 3.

425 A stump bedstead, feather bed, and bolster.

426 A mattrass, 3 blankets, and a coverlet.

427 A washstand and fittings, towel horse, chair, piece of carpet.

428 A mahogany chest of drawers, bed-side table, and a toilet glass.

## COACHMAN'S ROOM.

429 A stump bedstead, feather bed and bolster, 2 blankets and a coverlet.

430 A painted chest of drawers, deal table, chair, and a hanging glass.

## SERVANT'S BED ROOM.

431 A French bedstead, hair mattrass, and chintz hangings.

432 A feather bed, bolster, pillow, 3 blankets, and 2 coverlids.

433 Three chairs, rush seats, 2 painted tables, and a toilet glass.

434 A mahogany chest of 5 drawers.

435 A ditto ditto.

436 A table and fittings, wire fender, brass mounted, fire irons, and a coal box.

437 Drab curtains for 2 windows, painted towel horse, night commode, and a painted chest of 5 drawers.

## SERVANT'S BED ROOM—No. 2.

438 A stump bedstead, feather bed, bolster, and 2 coverlets.

439 A similar lot.

440 Three blankets, 2 chairs, and a towel horse.

441 A washing stand and fittings, dressing table, toilet glass.

442 An elm chest of drawers, deal towel horse, soap box, lock and key, tin foot bath, and 2 clothes baskets.

## HOUSEKEEPER'S ROOM.

443 A wire fender and standards, fire irons, coal box, hearth brush, a copper tea kettle, and two pieces of oil cloth.
444 A Brussels carpet, 21 ft. by 15, and a rug.
445 An easy chair, stuffed and covered in linen, deal table and cover.
446 Six chairs, cane seats and loose cushions, and 3 painted chairs, rush seats.
447 A pair of green damask window curtains, long brass rod, and a mahogany table, 2 flaps.
448 Two tea trays and 3 waiters, brass pan, two tin tea kettles, and a pair of copper scales.
449 Seven tin canisters, 2 coffee biggins, hanger and shade, Dutch oven, beer can, pair of nippers, 2 brass candlesticks, flat candlestick, snuffers and tray, a mahogany knife box, and 20 pieces of cutlery.
450 Three spa ornaments.

## SERVANTS' HALL.

451 A strong polished elm dining table, 16 ft. by 3 ft.
452 Three ditto forms, and a stool.
453 A table covered with baize, 3 Windsor chairs, iron fender, an, fire irons.
454 An elm cupboard, fitted with drawers.
455 A square table, 2 beer cans, tea tray, 4 horns, 2 salt cellars, box 8 pieces of cutlery, and a pierced fender.

## KITCHEN.

456 A deal table, 9 ft. by 3 ft., and 6 Windsor chairs.
457 Two small deal tables, 2 wood coal boxes, and an 8-day clock.
458 A copper stock pot, and 9 stew pans.
459 A ditto frying pan, 2 beer cans, and 4 saucepans.
460 Two moulds, 3 saucepans and lids, preserving pan, baking sheet, and cutlet pan.
461 A large fish kettle, and a pot.
462 A fish kettle, and a turbot kettle.
463 A return iron fender, set of fire irons, and a large deal meat screen, lined with tin.
464 Two large copper tea kettles, and a warming pan.

## LARDER.

465 A stone mortar and wood pestle and cover, on a clock.

466 Two meat safes and 4 seives, chopping board, paste board, and a rolling pin.

467 A set of scales and weights.

468 Nine white basins, bread pan, jelly stand, 2 wine coolers, teapot, and various ware.

469 Five mats, wood coal box, pair of steps, umbrella stand, footbrush and scraper.

## SCULLERY.

470 A strong deal table, and a set of steps.

471 Wood coal boxes, wood bowl, 2 chopping blocks, 2 dish tubs, and 4 sieves.

472 A stone salting pan, 4 wood chopping boards, clothes basket, stool and a slop pail.

473 A gridiron, 3 coffee pots, steamer, pudding tin, iron pan and skimmer, and 5 tin dish covers.

474 Ten tin dish covers.

475 A coffee roaster, 3 basting spoons, flesh fork, meat safe, 4 choppers, baking tin, tin can, chop tongs and iron stand, plate, iron stew pan, and a small saucepan.

476 A soup ladle, bottle jack, 6 candlesticks, 3 spits, 7 iron saucepans, gridiron, dripping pan and stand.

477 Two large tin steamers, brass tops, and one ditto smaller.

## BUTLER'S PANTRY.

478 A handsome or-molu sideboard lamp for two lights, with shades.

479 A gilt candle lamp with shade, and an oil lamp, with blue china pillar.

480 Three camphine lamps, shades, &c.

481 Two camphine lamps, 2 reflectors, 2 reading lamps, and a bronzed pillar and lamp.

482 Two wedgwood water bottles, and 2 Oriental china hot water plates.

483 A bronzed tea urn, a mahogany luncheon tray with handles, and 2 mahogany knife boxes.

484 Two pair of carvers, 6 dessert knives, and 8 knives and forks, buck horn handles.

485 Eighteen pewter hot water plates.

486 Three chairs, piece of oil cloth, mat, fender and fire irons, and a mahogany table.

487 Two butler's mahogany trays and stands, and 2 tea trays.

488 Three trays, 4 small oil lamps, 2 beer cans, and a napkin press.

489 Eighteen richly gilt dessert plates.

490 A mahogany medicine chest, 2 inkstands, and letter weight.

## CHINA AND GLASS.

491 Two quart and 4 pint cut decanters.

492 Two quart decanters, 2 water bottles, and a butter tub and stand.

493 Two water jugs, and two ground glass sugar basins.

494 Three claret decanters, and a pickle vase, and 7 custard cups.

495 Eighteen cut finger glasses, and 15 wine coolers.

496 Nineteen blue finger glasses and 4 claret glasses

497 Twenty champagne glasses, and 11 liqueur glasses.

498 Forty-seven wine glasses—various.

499 Twelve ale glasses, 10 tumblers, 20 wines, and 18 ice plates.

500 A blue and white china breakfast and tea service; viz., nine breakfast cups and saucers, 12 tea cups and saucers, 12 coffee cups and saucers, 2 dishes, 12 plates, 2 muffin plates and covers, butter dish and cover, 6 egg cups, slop pail, and milk jug.

501 Part of a tea and coffee service, white and gold edge, 4 jugs, green glass flower vase, water jug, hyacinth glass, 20 lamp glasses, and 5 oil lamps.

502 A blue and white dinner service, consisting of soup tureen, cover and stand, 4 vegetable dishes, covers and stands, 3 sauce tureens, covers and stands, fish drainer, 4 pie dishes, 18 soup plates, 53 meat plates, and 36 pie plates.

503 A handsome French china dessert service, painted in flowers and richly gilt, consisting of a centre, 10 compotiers, 2 ice pails, 2 sugar vases and covers, and 24 plates.

504 A cut glass centre dish, and 4 small ditto.

505 Part of Wedgwood dinner and dessert service, 170 pieces various.

*End of Twenty-first Day's Sale.*

# TWENTY-SECOND DAY'S SALE.

On TUESDAY, the 30th day of AUGUST, 1859,

AT ONE O'CLOCK PRECISELY.

## LAUNDRY, &c.

LOT

506 A patent mangle, by Wilkinson.

507 An ironing stove and piping, shovel and tongs.

508 A wood coal box, 7 flat irons, 3 deal clothes horses, deal table, bench and stool, ironing blanket, and mangle cloth, 2 iron stands, ironing board and blanket.

509 A saw, hatchet, wood bench, shovel, clothes horse, pail, deal box, carriage jack, and dog's house.

510 Five paint pots and brushes, 5 oil cans, paint stone and knife, 2 pitch pots, iron ladle, rope and pullies.

511 Seven iron bound pails, iron stove, coal box and tongs.

512 A coal box, bench, saddle horse, 2 rugs, table, chair, 2 halters, 4 brushes, and an oil lamp.

## UNDER GALLERIES.

513 A high wire fender, deal table, 2 flaps, and a chair.

514 A mahogany picture case, 2 doors, a rosewood ditto, and a hair brush.

515 A table, 2 picture cases, and boxes, various, and sundry panes of glass.

516 A fire-wood box, paper hangers' bench, 2 baskets, and wood coal box.

517 Twelve scaffold planks, 8 poles, boards, ropes, pulleys, and blocks.

518 A wheelbarrow, 4 trestles, 2 tubs, and 4 painted pedestals.

519 A quantity of glazed frame work, and part of a conservatory.

520 A set of flue tools, shovels, coal boxes, hammers, and implements connected with stoves.

521 Two ladders.
523 A carpenters' level, a flight of steps 16 tiers, and a stone truck.
524 An iron windlass and frame.
525 New doors and frame work.
526 A quantity of plasterers' tools, wheelbarrows, &c.
527 A large gilt picture frame.
528 A deal table, bench, knife board, stand and steps, 2 mats, and sundries.
529 An old stove, and various tin and iron.

## GARDEN IMPLEMENTS AND OUT DOOR EFFECTS.

530 Three spades, a shovel, 3 forks, pick axe, stock axe, garden line and pair of shears.
531 Daisy rake, 3 small rakes, 5 hoes, pair of small shears, edging iron and turf beater.
532 Two scythes, extra blade, mallet, trowel, and grass barrow.
533 A small barrow, grindstone, and about 25 dozen of pots various.
534 A similar lot.
535 Four line posts, and quantity of fire wood, hard.
536 A cart and a hand barrow.
537 A garden engine with hose.
538 Seven flower pots, set of steps and a small timber truck.
539 A carriage ladder, 2 corn bins, and chaff box.
540 Eleven small flower tubs, 13 flower shapes, and 5 stages.
541 Five wood snow shovels, 2 forks, shovel, 6 seakale pots, nest of seed shelves, 4 baskets, pair of shears, and turfing iron.
542 A painted corn bin, ladder, set of steps, and 2 box frames.
543 A ladder with 21 rounds.
544 An iron roller, with balance handles.
545 A nailing ladder, shovel, set of steps, and a gun.
546 A short ladder, 6 flower sticks, 5 hand lights, and 5 watering pots.
547 Two thermometers, set of steps, and brass syringe.
548 Two iron garden seats.
549 Two large iron flower pots.
550 Two thermometers, step ladder, rake, scraper and flower stand.
551
552 Two Camellias, 5 Azaleas, and 30 pots various.
553 Six Azaleas, and 40 pots of various plants.
554 Fifty pots of plants various.

555 Fifteen Myrtles.
556 Fifteen ditto, in tubs.
557 Two Cacti, 1 Hydrangea, and 4 Veronicas.
558 An iron stove and piping, and a flower stage.
559 Two work benches, 2 saw benches and a set of steps.
560 A similar lot.
561 Two oak gate posts and a quantity of old wood.
562 About 136 ft. of red deal, and 12 elm boards.
563 An iron vice, about a half cwt. of nails, various sizes, and some screws.
564 About 126 ft. of spruce deal.
565 A nest of shelves, 2 scaffold boards, plank, and a block, 23 ft.
566

---

567 A pair of mahogany picture easels.
568 A mahogany picture frame, 4 ft. by 3, and a rosewood ditto, with doors.
569 A mahogany music stand, 4 brass sconces.
570 A large Spanish mahogany picture screen, on castors and sunk handles.
571 Two ditto ditto, double, on castors and brass handles.
572 A pair of library steps, with banisters, and a rosewood picture screen.
573 A deal picture case, mahogany ditto, and a carved and gilt frame, 26 in. by 20.
574 Fourteen laths, 5 ft. 6 long, and 8 glazed sashes and gilt mouldings.
575 An ebony picture frame, 6 ft. 6 by 3 ft. 6, and a small one glazed, and a large gilt frame.
576 Six screen mounts, quantity of gilt ornaments, and a glass frame
577 Twelve French castors, plans of Thirlestane House, and various wood work.
578
579
580

## STATUARY FIGURES, BUSTS, &c. IN GARDEN.

581 *A fine antique* BRONZE BUST—MARCUS AURELIUS.
582 A DITTO DITTO—NERO.
583 A pair of large terra cotta vases, carved in relief—*called the Northwick vases.*
584 An antique marble bust of Cicero.
585 A ditto ditto—Augustus when young
586 *A very fine* MARBLE BUST of ALEXANDER, colossal size.
587 A DITTO DITTO—ARIADNE.
588 An antique marble bust—Augustus.
589 A small whole length figure of Venus with the apple, in terra cotta.
590 A marble bust of Faustina.
591 A terra cotta tazza, 2 ft. 9 in diameter.
592 An antique marble bust—Antonia Agrippa.
593 A ditto ditto—Agrippina.
594 A stone figure of BACCHUS, 4 ft. 6 high.
595 An antique marble bust of Septimus Geta.
596 A fine antique Head of Venus, in alabaster.
597 A marble Head of Aristotle.
598 A marble Head of Jean Jaques Rousseau.
599 A pair of terra cotta vases, 3 ft. high.
600 A fine stone figure THORWALDSEN'S SHEPHERD, 5 ft. in height.
601 A ditto ditto, HEBE, 5 ft. 6 high.
602 A pair of terra cotta vases.
603 Two antique marble heads.
604 A pair of plaster busts, and a pair of terra cotta ditto.
605 A pair of figures in Roman cement, of Tragedy and Comedy.
606 An antique marble Head of Julia Severi, and another of Marcus Aurelius.
607 A large terra cotta flower pot.
608 A large TORSO, in Roman cement.
609 A pair of stone vases.
610 A pair of terra cotta ditto, 3 ft. 6 high.
611 A set of 4 cleverly modelled stone figures of the Elements, on stone pedestals.
612 An antique marble bust, on a cippus.

613 A large figure, in Roman cement—THE DANCING FAWN.
614 A ditto ditto—THE DISCOBOLUS.
615 A marble head of Cicero, and another of Augustus
616 A large figure of the DISCOBOLUS, in Roman cement.
617 A large plaster figure.
618 A small marble Head of Plotina, and another of Julia.
619 A figure with a dolphin, in Roman cement, forming a fountain.
620
621
622

FINIS.

CPSIA information can be obtained
at www.ICGtesting.com
Printed in the USA
LVHW100905250223
740367LV00002B/174

9 783382 305772